BINARY
Code

Rebecca Sherwin
&
D H Sidebottom

Copyright © 2016

Rebecca R Sherwin & Dawn H Sidebottom

All rights reserved.

This book is a work of fiction. Characters, places, events and incidents are a product of the author's imagination. Any resemblance to real persons, living or dead, is purely coincidental.

Please do not copy, alter or distribute Binary Code. By purchasing this content, you agree to abide by copyright laws and will not copy, trade, pirate or replicate any of the content within this book.

If you have not purchased Binary Code by Rebecca Sherwin & D H Sidebottom, or it was not purchased for you, please return it to the seller and purchase your own copy.

Thank you.

We would like to thank everyone who has played a part in the making, promotion, and release of Binary Code.

We'd also like to thank all the twisted little darklings who purred with glee and smiled towards the devils on their shoulders when we announced we'd be writing together. The response was amazing and we are so grateful for the support.

We are both insanely proud of what became of Binary Code, and as a result—a product of the solid friendship we've found and the number of times we said, "that's exactly what I was thinking!"—our crazies will be colliding again.

Thank you to our readers, for giving this deviant duo a chance. We're beyond excited to let this baby loose on the world.

Love,

Rebecca and Dawn

xo

Warning

This book contains trigger scenes for some.

Please hold on to your heart, and hide your breath in your lungs.
You're about to be mind-fucked.

Sometimes it's not always about what you can see or hear but what's under the hood of a game that's most impressive. Between those thousands and thousands of lines of code, magic happens. Sometimes the most amazing feats of wizardry happen without you even noticing.
~ Rob Manuel

Prologue
HARLEY

My heart stampeded. The roar of blood pounded in my ears. Tears fell from my eyes as I stared in horror, the sharp sting after not blinking for so long making my vision blur at the edges. The tightness in my chest grew and my lungs started to constrict as the bile that was stuck in my throat obstructed the oxygen needed to fill them.

I couldn't look away from the grotesque form laid out before me like a gift—which in a way I suppose he was, his very last breath an offering to me.

His dead eyes fixed on my horror-stricken ones, the blank stare mirroring mine. His head was bent at an angle that couldn't, *shouldn't*, be possible, the severe twist in his neck making his chin rest perfectly between his shoulder blades.

My head shook so hard the impact made my body tremble, my muscles constricting to stabilise the rattle in my bones. My jaw clenched when my teeth started to chatter. I was so cold, the icy panic and reality of what lay before me seeping into the marrow of my bones and making me numb. The bass of the music beat in time with my heart, the sharp notes of whatever the singer was saying piercing my soul with every screech and squeal, every sensual hum that filled the void in her song. But not in me. I felt hollow. I felt empty; I felt like a part of me had evaporated when he died. When he was murdered. His life stolen from him before my eyes.

"Harley."

I blinked once, twice, as he called me again. His voice, low and seductive, firm and unforgiving, sent goose bumps to flare over my skin and burn against the coldness I felt. Finally, my stare shifted to find the source of the soft, coaxing voice. Eyes void of remorse bore into me, stealing the breath I was desperately trying to draw. He held me captive in his gaze, keeping me frozen to the spot, until he took a step towards me. On instinct, I shuffled back.

"No." I wasn't sure if I had even managed to speak the word or if my mind had just ordered it because I knew I should want him to stay away.

Nothing was real. Nothing made sense. But then, in so many ways, it did. While my eyes were struggling to define, my mind was sighing in relief. Every single one of my unanswered questions were finally satisfied. So many things that had made me doubt myself slotted into place, yet, still none of them made any sense. The conflict between my eyes and my brain was making me nauseous, and my stomach roiled as I fought to keep a retch contained.

"Let me..."

My head shook harder and I lifted my hands from where they rested on my stomach, attempting to stop him getting any closer. Of course he didn't obey my silent command...had I expected him to? *Did I even want him to?* In my desperation to figure this out, rationalise what was happening, and force my mind to catch up to grant me some mercy, I needed to look away. I needed to not see, like I had been doing for so long. I needed the ignorance that once felt like a niggling ache for the truth; now it felt like I was being trampled by my own stupidity. They say ignorance is bliss...I could attest to that. I should have run while I had the chance.

My eyes ventured from him to my hands. Blood. So much blood. It coated my skin, dripping down my wrists and onto the floor. Flesh was buried deep under my fingernails, and a solitary pubic hair protruded from the edge of my thumbnail.

The bile that had been stuck in my throat spewed with the contents of my stomach and my knees buckled, forcing me to crumble in on myself. My hands slapped onto the floor as another wave of vomit burst from me. My stomach churned and water dripped from my eyes as my sanity broke and I screamed with every single heave of devastation.

Shoes came into my line of sight and I scuttled back, huddling myself into the wall as I tried to back away from him. I was trapped between his menacing form and the wall that felt like cotton against his frightening glare. I knew he wouldn't hurt me, he would have done it already, right? But it didn't stop the panic now I'd seen what he *could* do…and it didn't stop me glancing behind him, around him, above him. Anything to make sense of what was happening.

"You're hurt," he said gently, lifting his hands quickly to placate me as he dropped to crouch before me. "Let me help you."

Me.

But which one? Who was going to help me? Who was going to come to my rescue, and could I let them?

A wave of pain made my breath catch and my hands instinctively made to grab my belly. It was then I realised the blood that covered my hands was mine. Trickling. Pumping out with every beat of my heart. Soaking into my clothes as the adrenaline kicked in and told me to run. *Where have you been, adrenaline? I could have used this warning months ago.* The gash continued to seep and I became consciously aware of the pang of copper, the metallic smell so potent I could taste it. The pain. God, the pain. What had happened to me? How had I got here?

Out of it all…the dead man hideously still staring at me. The cruel break in my sanity. The vicious tremor racking my bones. The deafening rush of blood in my ears. The rapidly dimming double vision. The music that continued to pound, over and over, like a ticking time bomb. It had been counting down for some time—I realised that now. The few remaining grains of sand tumbled into the funnel to settle on a discarded pile of morality and with them, my mind began to slip. It was the sight of my own blood that forced my brain to offer me a reprieve and swallow me in the depths of unconsciousness.

Blackness consumed me as strong arms pulled me in.

One
HARLEY

Six Months Earlier

Art was my passion. Fashion not so much. Not at all. Stand me in front of Mona Lisa, or ask me about The Persistence of Memories and I'd be at home, at ease and more than adequate at holding my own. Put me in a dress, and I forgot how to breathe, how to stand, how to hold myself amongst my peers and colleagues. Bottom line: I hated dresses. I was more of a wing it and slob it girl; leggings, jeans and t-shirts were my comfort zone. However, the small but popular gallery I owned required more than my comfy clothes.

I plucked at the tight red silk strangling my figure as if it wanted to suffocate the life out of me in revenge for having to sit against my hot skin.

Closing my eyes for a second, I fantasised about the moment I could take my leave, return to my bubble of solitude, and slip into my usual jeans and t-shirt.

"Stop fidgeting," Evan, my best friend, chastised as he took my nervous fingers in his hand and squeezed tight, passing me a flute of champagne at the same time. "You've done this a million times. What's eating you tonight?"

What was eating me tonight? I wasn't sure, but something in my gut told me I had to get out of here and run. Fast. My instincts had been in overdrive all day as I prepared for tonight, and as I took another glance around the room I still couldn't put my finger on exactly what had me so on edge.

My art gallery was my sanctuary, the tranquillity of the different features and colours decorating each wall calming the chaos that constantly travelled around my body. The varying scenes that I usually found myself sinking into and pretending my life was normal, ordinary, no longer offered me their refuge. Tonight each sectioned area felt like a prison, a trap that would suck me in and never let me go. I'd never felt unwelcome in the only place I called home, but tonight I felt like the outcast. Why? I didn't know.

"I'm fine," I lied, knowing Evan would see right through me, so I tossed the champagne back before he had the chance to analyse me some more.

"Miss Davids!"

Both myself and Evan groaned when Bill Clancy's high-pitched tone vibrated in our eardrums. He had a voice that reminded me of nails on a chalkboard and, unfortunately, I'd been subjected to more conversations with him than I wanted.

"Who the hell invited him?" Evan grumbled in my ear, his irritation as paramount as mine.

Plastering on a fake smile, I turned to face the round and sickly pale face of the creepiest politician in history. "Mr Clancy, such a pleasure to see you again."

His smile was wide and I cringed when he planted a wet kiss to my cheek, his large belly pressing into me as he moved to my other cheek. "The pleasure, as always, is mine, Harley."

Evan rolled his eyes and then winked and wandered off. I glared at him, the traitor, before moving away from Bill's unsettling molestation.

He looked around the room and then turned back to me. "The collection is magnificent. There are quite a few pieces I am considering purchasing. Is the artist here tonight?" Once again he looked around the room, his eyes hunting for his next prey.

Almost guiltily, I nodded. "She is. Would you like me to introduce you, Mr Clancy?"

I cringed inwardly when his hand settled at the base of my spine as I led him over to Jemima, the backless dress I had stupidly chosen to wear making his touch more nauseating.

"Have you thought anymore about my offer?" he whispered in my ear, leaning closer to me than was necessary, and comfortable.

Bile swirled in my stomach and I snatched another glass of champagne off the tray of a passing waiter. "Unfortunately, at the moment, I don't have the time to give a relationship the attention it would need, Mr Clancy."

I felt him stiffen beside me. His fingers that were still touching my naked skin twitched with irritation at my obvious lie. I thought it sounded pretty respectful for a brush off. By *relationship*

Clancy meant *no strings attached fucking.* And I was far from interested in anything that meant I'd be disrespected, disregarded, and bouncing around in bed on a disproportionately sized chauvinist with a huge belly, an ego to match, and an even bigger mouth that meant my reputation would soon end up in tatters.

He didn't reply but I sensed his ire as we approached a group of people surrounding Jemima. She turned to me and smiled as I slipped into the small throng and made introductions. "Jemima, I'd like you to meet Bill Clancy MP. Mr Clancy, this is Jemima Danvers, the featured artist for tonight's exhibition."

Recognition flashed in her pretty blue eyes, Bill's reputation obviously preceding him.

My teeth sank into my lower lip when Bill slipped his arm around my waist and shuffled in closer to me as he took Jemima's hand and lifted it to his mouth. "Such a pleasure, Miss Danvers. You have a beautiful gift." I wasn't sure if he was referring to her art or her chest when his eyes slid down her body, greedily eating her up.

I stepped to the side but Bill held me tight, his fingers digging into my hip and making me wince slightly. My teeth slipped out of my lip and clamped together as I attempted to calm myself, the nausea swiftly becoming a problem.

The cells in my blood started popping, the deep chill settling into my bones turning into a bigger problem than the queasiness...hunger. *Not tonight. Christ, not tonight!*

"Miss Davids."

My gaze swung to a man stood beside Jemima. An involuntary gasp left me when my eyes met his. He had the strangest eyes I'd ever seen, one dark green almost brown, and the other a crystalline blue. I narrowed my eyes, intensifying my stare. I stared rudely for the longest time, the deep complex irregularity mesmerising me. I'd never been so hypnotised by such uniqueness. Yet it wasn't the uncommon eye colour that captured me, but the glint of darkness that radiated from the stare holding mine. He was compelling and deterring all at once. I wanted to step back, turn around and run away, and yet I wanted to step closer. All the way closer, until I could make out every fleck of colour in his abominable eyes.

Forcing myself to blink, I snapped out of the trance and smiled, holding out a hand in offering. He took it, clamping his fingers around my wrist. I gasped when he tugged, snatching me away from Bill's hold. I stumbled in my heels but his other hand seized the top of my arm to steady me.

His fierce gaze looked down at me and he gave me the faintest of smiles. "I was hoping to steal you for a minute, Miss Davids."

My brain couldn't fire a single synapse, and I stood mutely staring up at him. He was tall, at least six feet four inches. His hard, lean body pressed against my soft form but it was the look in his eyes, the silent demand, that had me nodding. For some strange reason I felt manipulated, as if he had physically taken my chin between his fingers and moved my head up and down in agreement to his order.

His gaze snapped from mine and he turned to Bill. "Please excuse us, Bill."

Bill, as stunned as me, blinked and frowned as if he'd just been fucked over. No one addressed Bill Clancy as anything other than Mr Clancy. The man who had stepped in, muted me, and now wanted to 'steal' me for a minute couldn't have cared less about who he *stole* me from.

Not waiting for Bill to answer, he spun around abruptly and directed us across the room. He didn't stop until he had snatched two flutes of champagne from a passing waitress and was offering me a seat at an empty table in the corner.

I couldn't look away from him, my eyes locked onto the way he moved, the way he radiated such aggressive authority, the way his jaw clenched as if he was furious. His hand in mine felt hot, the touch sending bolts of electricity up my arm and into my brain, numbing it in shock.

My reaction to him didn't make any sense. I forced myself to pull my hand away.

He narrowed his eyes but gestured to the chair again. He wasn't going to take no for an answer, and curiosity would make me comply.

Grateful for the rest to my trembling legs, I sat heavily and continued to stare at him. Why was that all I was capable of around him?

"Carter." He finally introduced himself as he pulled his chair closer to mine and lowered his body down. His legs were so long he had to stretch them out, and he crossed them at the ankles. My eyes slid down him, taking in the way his trousers pulled against taut thighs and how the crisp white shirt hugged his defined stomach.

What the hell was wrong with me? I'd lost all motor skills, a puppet to his inexplicable influence over me.

"Carter...?" I prompted for his surname.

"Just Carter," he stated firmly. "You looked a little uncomfortable in Bill's custody so I offered you a way out."

Oh.

Relaxing slightly with his gallantry, I grimaced. "Yes, he is a..."

"Cunt."

The expletive was so sharp and full of belligerence that I couldn't help but gasp.

"Do you have the credentials to say such a thing?"

"Do I need a certificate of education to call a cat a cat?"

"Of course not."

"Then I can call a cunt a cunt."

I shivered. The way the expletive clipped from his mouth brought my gaze to the lips that said it. I licked mine in reaction and kept the bottom one between my teeth.

"Touché. I was going to say persistent, but we'll agree on your observation."

"How very gracious of you." His fierce gaze softened for a second and he smiled very faintly. "See, we already have so much in common."

I nodded, unsure of what to make of his statement. "We have other things in common aside from our dislike of Bill?"

He took a sip of the champagne he was holding and I watched his Adam's apple bob as the liquid slid down his throat. His chin was square, and closely shaven, but it was his full lips that drew my gaze once more when he moved the glass away. As if aware of my bizarre fascination with him, he slowly turned his head until he was staring right at me. His eyes dropped to my mouth and his tongue swept across his lips, collecting the champagne that coated them. "I'm sure we can find something, Miss Davids."

My bones shivered, and I was horrified that I couldn't hide my reaction to his deep voice.

Taking a much needed sip of my own drink, I forced it down and smiled. "So, Mr Carter..."

"Just Carter," he offered with a slight raise of his eyebrow.

"So, Carter," I rectified. "What is it that I can do for you?"

His lips twitched and I wasn't sure if he was amused or irritated. Placing his glass down on the table, he leaned forwards and rested his elbows on his knees. He was so close to me that I could feel the gentle fan of his warm breath on my cheek and I shivered impulsively. "We have two choices, Miss Davids."

I tipped my head. "We do?"

"Hmm." He swept a long finger over his bottom lip and my eyes dropped as if magnetised to watch the hypnotic movement. His gaze lifted and fixed on mine, the deep swirl of green crashing with the soft glint of blue. "We can either go around the back of your impressive gallery and fuck in the alley, or we can fuck right here, in front of all these egotistical cunts."

My eyes grew wider and wider with every one of his words, until they watered with dryness and shock.

"But I have to say," he continued, his gaze piercing through me to gage my reaction. "I'm not so sure the rats will take kindly to you panting and writhing in their usually quiet neighbourhood."

"What the…?"

He smirked, clearing his throat with nothing but arrogance, and leaned back into his chair once again. "And I'm quite positive Bill will appreciate the sight of your tight little ass when I bend you right over this table and slide down those silky black knickers I know you're wearing."

As if expecting my assault, he didn't flinch when my palm connected with his right cheek. His head barely moved although I knew I'd hit him hard, and his skin reddened instantly.

Unable to find the words, I huffed and stood on jelly legs.

"You'll grow to love me, Miss Davids," he laughed as I strode away.

"You have no idea who I am, do you, Carter?" I muttered to myself, feeling his eyes on me until I rounded the corner.

My teeth were clenched with indignation, even if every single one of my nerve endings was buzzing with stimulation. I had never been so openly propositioned, and never in such a blunt manner. The glint of desire in his eyes, the raw sex that he exhumed and the straightforward way he had spoken should have turned my stomach with disgust, yet there was a rage in my blood that I hadn't felt for a very long time.

Evan rushed over to me and I sighed. The look on his face had me stiffening and soon forgetting the way my treacherous body had reacted to Carter's 'offer'.

"Benny," Evan growled, the concern in his eyes as he thrust his phone at me making my heartbeat stutter.

Evan, proficiently, directed Bill back into the throng of the other guests when he spotted him making a beeline for me.

"Ben." I lowered my voice as I turned my back on the room and manoeuvred around the thick red ropes that cordoned off a section of the gallery.

"Shit creek, Harl, and the paddle is well and truly fucking adrift!" Ben spluttered into the phone.

"Bring me up to date."

"Fuck!" he mumbled over the clicking of the keyboard. "I dunno, something is blocking me."

Frowning, I licked at my dry lips. "Have you merged the sequence?"

"It won't fucking let me!"

"Okay, calm down," I urged, drumming my fingers against my thigh as I subconsciously tapped at my own keyboard and mentally worked through the problem. "Are you sure you don't have a leech?"

"Well if I do he's fucking veiled. Shit, Harley. I have six hundred and forty-eight seconds to burrow. I'm fucked."

Closing my eyes, I dug my fingernails into my palm. "Link me in. Give me four."

"What? You're at the gallery."

"Well-" I cut myself short with a squeal as I ran through the building to the office at the back, the stupid heels that were already killing my feet making me slide on the polished floor. "I'll have to enter through here and pray I don't get a chaser."

"It's too risky, Harl. You can't!"

"I have to! It's a six point five, Ben. Are you willing to lose that?"

His huff said everything. "I'm sorry..."

"Don't. I'll fix it. Have you tied IPs?"

"Yeah, you should already be in."

The office was cool when I entered, the air-con that had been on full all night to accommodate for the full house making the empty room chilly, and I shivered as I hit the lights and powered up the PC.

"Five hundred and twenty-four, Harl," Ben muttered, the anxiety in his voice evident as I switched to speakerphone and placed the phone on the desk. "Where are you?"

Pulling up my chair, and silently thanking Evan for having me buy a new top-grade kit for the gallery when it powered up in seconds, I cracked my knuckles. I worked my way through the network, logged in and was chasing Ben's tail within ninety seconds. "I'm with you."

Four minutes later, we both let out a sigh of relief.

"Shit, what the fuck happened?" Ben asked.

Dropping back into my chair I wiped the sweat off my palms on my dress and blew out a breath. "Looked like a vortex. You had to twist it the other way."

"I tried, nothing worked."

"It doesn't make sense." I sighed, shaking my head in puzzlement. "It was a simple doorway; it should have opened easily."

"Hmm. Beats me. I got nothin'." I heard his chair creak as I listened to my own heartrate settle. "Listen, I'll clean up. Get back to the party."

Already shutting everything off, I nodded even though he couldn't see me. "Okay. Breakfast?"

"Sure thing. I owe you a waffle or two."

"Make it three and coffee, and I'll think about giving you your split."

He scoffed then ended the call.

"Nicely done."

I jumped at the low but rough voice behind me, spinning in the chair.

A cold sheet of anxiety washed over me when I saw Carter leaning against the doorframe, his arms crossed over his chest and a smirk on his lips.

"What the hell?" My arm flung across the desk to shut off the PC screen. "What are you doing here?"

He unpeeled his arms and pushed off the door. His eyes never left mine as he stalked across the room to me. My brain wouldn't work, the panic in my chest making my bones seize with the fear of how long he had been stood there and how much he'd seen.

"I'd heard how good you were, Harley, but I just thought it was exaggeration due to the fact that most of your clients want to screw you."

My mouth fell open and my neck creaked when I stared up at him looming over me. The darkness in his eyes transfixed me once again, the hypnotic way he held me hostage leaving me vulnerable and completely numb to the rage that should have been coming to the surface by now.

I flinched when he brought his hand to my face and trailed the tip of his finger across my cheekbone. "Quite the fiddler, aren't you?"

"What if I am?" I asked stupidly, my mind void of any coherent thought.

My instincts were lagging behind, the panic that was overwhelming me clashing with the way this strange man appeared to compel me so effortlessly. I was trying to figure out how much of a threat he posed, but all I could wonder was if he'd followed me here with the intent to seduce me, and found himself slamming into an entirely different hole. I prayed he had no understanding, that he was clueless and I was safe.

Slowly, he lowered to a crouch before me. His eyes left my gaze to watch his finger trail over the shell of my ear, and I gasped when he pinched the lobe. "Then I would say things could get real interesting."

Fear trickled through me and finally kick-started the adrenaline I needed to function. I tried to bolt but it was already impossible with him directly in front of me.

His hand shot from my ear and closed around my throat as he pinned me to the back of the chair.

"Now, now, no need to rush off so quickly."

"What do you want?" I hissed through the restriction on my windpipe.

His gaze lowered to my mouth when I spoke and then moved back to my eyes. "Hmm, there's an open question. What do I want, Harley Davids?" He smirked. "Cool name by the way. It's...amusing."

I glared at him, squirming beneath his hold as I tried to free myself from the severe grip he had on me. My pulse was thumping in my ears as my heart thudded against my ribcage, the perfect symmetry making the air pulsate around me. "I'm glad I can entertain you."

He chuckled. "Oh I'm sure we can find something more than your name to entertain us."

Every part of me froze when he slid his hand down my neck and pressed it to the centre of my breastbone, right above the swell of my breasts. His eyes glinted and he licked his lips when he saw my fear. My throat ached from his strict hold and I gulped for air.

"Now, here's my dilemma, Harley. I have a job to do, but what I really want to do is slide up your dress, tear off those pretty little knickers and find out if you're as tight as I imagine."

I shook my head, gulping at the lingering tightness in my throat and the phantom fingers still curled around it. "Please don't."

He blinked, his brow creasing slightly. "Oh, don't worry, I won't take you until you offer it. And believe me, you will offer yourself to me. In fact, I have no doubt that you'll be fucking begging for it."

His arrogance made me fight but he was too strong, pressing me to the chair and refusing me the chance to flee.

Then, unexpectedly, he stood upright and his menacing closeness disappeared. His smile was cold and the heat in his eyes did nothing to warm the chill radiating from him as he took another step back.

"Until next time, babe."

And with a wink he was gone, leaving me staring in shock at the doorway he disappeared through.

I took one deep breath after another, trying to sedate my erratic breathing. The chaos had returned, buzzing in my mind until colour became black and white and sounds became white noise against a new sensation.

Craving.

Longing.

Needing.

"Harley."

I looked up to see Evan standing where Carter had been just moments ago. Evan knew everything, and Carter knew too much. My best friend, the man I'd known since we were kids, when I would run around shooting the bad guys from the back of my motorbike, and he would follow behind me waiting for the game to end, knew every time I took a breath...and yet, he'd never been under my skin, not like...

"What happened?"

"I'm fine," I lied. "I'm fine," I repeated, before releasing a defeated breath and dropping my chin to my chest. Shame overwhelmed me when I muttered, "Cloud."

I heard Evan sigh with the single word, but his fingers slipped in mine and he smiled softly at me as I looked up at him. "Come on, let's get you sorted."

Tears blurred his face when I nodded, and I tightened my grip on him as he tugged me off the chair. His lips pressed to my forehead, his complete love for me reflected in that simple action. "Love you, Harl."

"Forever," I whispered as he led me out of the building and once again cared for me like no other ever could.

Two
CARTER

Women. I'd never much needed one before. Sure, I fucked as often as the next single dude with charm and a smile, but that was where my respect for women ended. If they jumped in my bed, they could have me for a few hours and then they'd become irrelevant. No pillow talk, no breakfast, and no kiss goodbye when I sent them on their way.

I'd never killed a woman before, either. Seems like a weird observation to make, right? Not for me. I had as many kills under my belt as I did notches on my bedpost. When I'd received the order, and payment, to take out one Harley Davids, I'd sniggered at the name imagining it was a MC douchebag from bumfuck USA who had pissed off a rich guy by breaking bottles on his precisely clipped lawn. Never in a million years had I expected to stumble upon *female* Harley Davids, of Alconbury, Cambridgeshire. She was no bumfuck, although one look at her and I'd imagined fucking her delectable arse, and now, hours later, I was still imagining fucking her, while trying to figure out *why* her death had earned a price tag. I didn't usually care about the why. I stormed in, fired one shot, and got the fuck out a few grand better off. I didn't kill for sport. I didn't even kill for a living. I killed because I had an insatiable desire to do it, and that was reason enough for me. I'd given myself a solid alibi that would be sure to have my back for decades to come. I owned Chimera, a four-story club that had been nothing but a childhood dream, and now it stood proud against the most well-respected establishments in the country, and had planted my name at the top of nightclub-moguls' hit-lists nationwide. If only they knew I had access to every hitman's archive on both sides of the Atlantic and beyond.

Harley Davids...the name left a sour taste on my tongue, and created an aggressive stir in my pants. This was why I didn't involve myself with women beyond a quick suck, a quicker fuck and shoving them out the door before my cum had even dried on their thighs. This was why I didn't kill women. Because, somehow, the two confused themselves, the very fibres of my being and everything that moulded me into the man I was, collided until I didn't know if I was a thirty-three-year-old man who had made it, or a young boy who wondered if he ever would.

Dragging my hands through my hair, I switched the light on in the apartment I lived in at the top of Chimera and stared out at the city in the distance. Then with a sigh, I slammed my fist into the console beside the door and watched as the shutters blocked the world out. I could smell her on me; lemons, cherries and vanilla that made my mouth water like a diabetic in a bakery. My tongue flexed against the roof of my mouth when I remembered wanting to suck on the flesh of her neck, lick the vein that had pulsed in fear when her instincts told her to run. She'd been right to be afraid of me. I'd been there to kill her...but I couldn't do it.

Why couldn't I fucking do it?

Stripping out of the jacket and folding it onto the back of the sofa as I crossed the living space, I tried to find a reason for why I'd let her live when I'd found—created—the opportunity to end her swiftly. I grabbed a bottle of beer from the fridge and popped the cap, leaning against the counter and taking a mouthful, while my free hand unbuttoned my shirt and untucked it from my trousers. Brown eyes that reminded me of the chocolate ice cream I wasn't allowed as a kid filled my vision. Harley's fucking eyes. The way they'd widened in shock when I seized her throat. The way they'd filled with tears when I told her we'd be fucking, and she'd be damn well begging for it.

"Fucking hell," I groaned, closing my eyes and tipping my head back.

I should have fucked her tonight. I knew if I had, if she had let me, I would have been able to kill her. I always lost interest after I'd won the fight. If there was no challenge, if I'd won the game I'd created without disclosing the rules, the object of my need to dominate became boring. Redundant. She would have become insignificant and I would have been able to do the job I'd been paid in advance to carry out.

Had my employer seen this? Had he foreseen the effect Harley would have on me? Did she have this effect on everyone around her?

And why was I fucking angry about it? Why did the thought of another man taking her life, when it was my job to do so, make me so angry that the neck of the bottle snapped in my savage grip? I needed to *get* a grip. I needed to get over this, and I needed to try again tomorrow.

I wouldn't fail. I never failed.

Slamming what was left of my beer on the counter, I stormed through the apartment to take a shower, pulling on a fresh suit when I was done, ignoring the hard-on that had turned into a desperate horny teenager vying for some attention. I headed out of the apartment, taking the private lift downstairs to where Saturday night in Chimera was buzzing. Bodies writhed against each other, sweat mixed with alcohol and adrenaline from the heavy bass pounding from wall to wall and floor to ceiling. The DJ stood at his decks, bouncing his arms up and down to the beat of the music and the strobe lighting that burst from every inch of the club. It was an epileptic's biggest nightmare, and everything junkies craved from a high. The crowd chanted, waitresses dressed in little black dresses with belts of liquor and stacks of shot glasses hanging around their hips fluttered their eyelashes and tempted punters into spending more money, and the bouncers stood in the corners watching for pricks behaving badly, and women trying to earn more than a free drink.

"Boss," Tim said, shaking my hand across the bar and shouting over the music. "The usual?"

I nodded, leaning my forearms on the bar top as he grabbed a glass and reached for the bottle of Johnnie Walker, pouring a healthy double-measure and then some, over ice.

"Busy night? I haven't seen you much tonight."

"Ah, I was upstairs for most of it," I lied.

"It's been good."

He didn't need to tell me; I knew our new plans would roll out successfully. This was my forte, my speciality, the only thing I lived for when I wasn't balls deep in a warm cunt or drowning blissfully in blood. I treated my staff well; I treated every single person in this club with respect, as if I were their equal. All in the name of keeping the mask in place. So when I decided to try different music, when I planned themed nights and replenished the alcohol stock with new brands and fresh labels, people flocked to offer their support; they brought their friends with them and if someone were to say, *"hey, did you know Carter is an assassin?"* I'd have hundreds of people to turn to for a character defence guaranteed to clear my name before I even made it to the station. That's not to say I wasn't careful; I was an obsessive son of a bitch, a germaphobe, a clean-freak. There was a way to do things, and that way was to leave not a single breadcrumb or shred of DNA.

I spotted the flash of a phone screen across the bar and smiled when I saw a woman sitting on a bar stool, nursing a cosmopolitan. Well made, judging by the bright shade of pink and the slice of lime garnishing the glass.

"You know it's dangerous to drink alone, don't you, sweetheart?" I said, approaching her from behind and sliding onto the stool next to her.

I needed to be this close to her to see if she was drunk, to see if it made me more of a fucking arsehole than I already was for hitting on a drunk woman.

"My friend was sick and had to leave," she said, not making eye contact as she continued to text. "I'm trying to get hold of my boyfriend to come and collect me."

"No taxi?"

Rolling her eyes, she finally trained them on me. "So it's dangerous to sit in a bar and enjoy a cocktail, yet it's okay to step outside and hail a taxi, completely unaware whether I'll make it home or die in a ditch?"

"Good answer," I said, showing genuine approval as I let my gaze travel her lithe body. "Dancer?"

"Gymnast."

"Drunk?"

"Barely."

"Barely?"

She winked. "I'm Irish."

"Ah." I hummed. "Then I think the luck o' the Irish found us both tonight."

"Is that right?"

Nodding, I answered, "Sure. Now, come on. Let me find you a licensed taxi. What kind of man would I be if I didn't commission a company to take vulnerable young women home from my club when they've been left behind and their boyfriend has fallen asleep with his X-Box on and his hands in his pants?"

"It's like you've been stalking me."

"I've been at this a while. You learn to read people."

The woman smirked, her bright red lips curving up on one side. She blinked slowly, seductively, before she licked her bottom lip and stood as I did. "Then you'd know there's no boyfriend."

"Oh, I know," I answered. "But I know why women play the boyfriend card."

"I hadn't looked at you at that point."

"Shallow?"

"You hadn't said much."

"Interesting."

"Maybe I don't want to go home just yet."

Bingo. This chick wasn't drunk, she had a perfect set of tits that I could imagine grinding my dick between, and she was pouting, ready for me to slide right between her lips. I'd picked her up and yet she believed she was the one charming me. Oh, naïve women.

"Another drink?" She shook her head. "A tour, perhaps?"

"I've seen all four floors tonight."

"Very well." So she'd been on the prowl. "Then you won't be interested to know there's a fifth?"

"Oh, I'm a keen architect. I know there's a fifth floor."

Slipping her hand into mine, she stared up at me with electric promise in her strobe-lit eyes. Gesturing to Tim, I told him to write off her tab, and led her through the club to the lift.

"I had fun," she said as I edged her over the threshold into the lift that would take her directly to the ground floor with no option to return to the penthouse. "We should do this again."

"I'm not sure your boyfriend would be too pleased about that."

"But-"

"I told you, sweetheart, I've been in the game a while," I scoffed, glancing at her in that way guaranteed to make her dislike herself as much as I did in the moment. "A man knows when another man has marked his territory."

"Excuse me?"

"Don't fight it. You've had your night of fun like I've had mine. Mind the smashed glass on your way out."

With that, I pushed the button and smiled in amusement when I watched her search for a button to hold the doors open. No such luck. The doors closed, the light above the lift signalled its descent and I shook my head as I turned and headed back into the apartment.

"She was hot."

"Jesus." I gripped a fistful of my hair and released a gust of breath when I realised I hadn't been broken in to. "Jobe, what the fuck?"

He shrugged. "Dude, she moaned like a fucking porn star."

"Well, you know I've got a monster cock. Poor girl didn't stand a chance."

"I thought you were splitting her in two. I was about to burst in with the Sellotape."

I laughed, and dropped to the sofa. "Would have made things more interesting, I guess."

"I thought so. I was sure I could hear the last porno you watched replaying in your mind."

"You're such a prick."

It was a lie. No, he was a prick, but there was no hate between us. We'd gone into business together when we were eighteen. Jobe stayed in the background, working on the logistics whereas I worked front of house, giving everyone a face to connect to Chimera and the empire it was quickly becoming. When I was out murdering for money, Jobe took over, and when he was off doing whatever it was he did—usually partaking in kinky shit and smoking weed—I took over. We swapped out frequently, and no one ever said shit. We ran this place like a single entity, picking up each other's slack and being the safety net when one screwed up and needed a little…assistance.

"Yeah, I've heard that before." He nodded at me, signalling at his hunger for information. "So how did it go?"

"It didn't. I think I'm going to have a little fun with this one." Jobe narrowed his eyes at me, but smiled. "I've been paid already, where's the harm in a little cat and mouse?"

"You're going to toy with your dinner before you boil it."

"Exactly. I'll get her well-seasoned and tenderised before I cut into her."

"Good thinking, man."

"That's why these pathetic cunts pay me…to do the shit they wish they could if they had a set of knackers."

"You ever just felt like turning on them? You know, giving them a taste of their own medicine?"

Shaking my head, I answered, "Nah. Not until one of them fucks me over. It's my release as much as it is their relief, you know?"

"You're a sick fuck."

"Takes one to know one." I stretched out, my neck cracking as I rolled it from side to side. "I'm hitting the sack."

"This early?"

"Yeah." I looked at my watch as I stood up. "The real fun begins tomorrow and I don't intend on wasting a second."

Three

HARLEY

"Morning," Evan grumbled as he took the seat at the table with Benny and me at our usual Sunday morning haunt, Barbara's.

Barbara's was a greasy spoon, the clientele often greasier than her food. But she made the meanest waffles this side of the river, and her tea was so strong you could stand your spoon up in it—how English tea should be.

"You look like shit, man," Ben commented, taking a sip of his tea and narrowing his eyes across the table at Evan.

Evan flicked a glance at me and nodded to Ben, who then swept his gaze my way.

He sighed and reached out, tapping the back of my hand. "Bad night, sweetheart?"

I nodded, shooting an apologetic smile at Evan. "Yeah."

"Oh, God." The guilt in Ben's gaze over last night's fiasco had me shaking my head quickly.

"Don't start."

"Shit, Harl. I have no idea what the hell happened." He chewed on his lip, leaning back into his chair when one of the waitresses brought over our food. She winked at Evan, both me and Benny quirking an eyebrow.

"Know her, do you?" Ben smirked when she walked away, the dramatic swing of her arse for Evan's benefit, I hoped. She was barking up the wrong tree if it was Ben she was hoping to snag.

Evan just rolled his eyes and took a bite of his toast. "Seriously, guys. We need to talk about whatever shit happened last night." He looked at Benny and frowned in thought. "Harley seems to think it was a leech, or at the very least, a deliberate block."

Ben nodded, diving into his full English. "Yeah, looks like it. Thank God Harley is shit hot at warrens 'cause I swear, any longer and I would have been buried in there. Did you find anything last night?"

Evan sighed, looking at me. I hated the disappointment reflecting back at me. "Harley wasn't much up to working last night."

Benny shrugged and nodded in understanding as he turned to me. "So, Miss Marple, what's the next step?"

"I've locked down as much as I could find, and I'll see what I can get from them later. But it definitely looks deliberate."

"Surely not the client?" Evan asked, nabbing a piece of my peach waffle with his fork and shoving it into his mouth before I could protest.

"That wouldn't make sense."

Benny dropped his gaze, and I narrowed my eyes on him. "Stranger things have happened. You have a theory?"

Clicking his tongue, he pushed his plate aside and grimaced. "Michael."

The blood in my veins froze and the waffle I'd eaten curdled in my stomach with the mention of his name. "What? Why...why would Michael get involved now? It's been..."

Evan grabbed my hand when I started to panic, the blood draining from my face and my body going into shock as the thunder of my heart banged against my chest bone. "It's okay, Harley. Benny isn't thinking." He glared at Ben, silently cautioning him.

Ben growled. "We all want that fucker buried in the past. But last night doesn't make sense. And the only hacker I know who can do that kind of work, especially chasing Harley's tail, is Michael."

"Michael is gone," I snapped, leaning back in my chair and scowling at Ben for even mentioning his name. "The debt was paid, in full." A shiver raced through me and Evan placed his hand over mine, giving me a tight squeeze. "He won't be back."

"He wouldn't fucking dare," Evan growled.

We fell silent and I pushed my plate away, my appetite gone and replaced by a different hunger.

"I have to go." The feet of my chair scraped on the dirty tiled floor as I quickly stood up.

Evan watched me closely. "Not again, Harl." There was a warning in his voice, but I ignored it as I snatched up my bag.

"I'll let you know if I get a footprint."

"Harley," Benny shouted after me but he didn't make any attempt to follow me.

They both knew where I would be for the next few hours. And they both knew better than to stop me.

Four
CARTER

Do you know how an assassin chooses his weapon? There were plenty of factors that affect it. How close did we want to get to the target? How intimate did we want to be? Did we want to hide out on a rooftop and shoot from tens of feet away? Did we want to stand in front of them and ram a bullet into their skull, watching brain explode, blood splatter, and listen to the thud of deadweight hit the ground? Did we want to feel the warmth leave them in a tsunami of blood, while we were granted the ultimate power of not only taking a life, but doing it with no personal motivation?

My methods varied. Sometimes, when I was one man, I would break into their house silently and let time and circumstance lead the way. When I was the other man, I planned each assassination to the second. I knew where the target would be; sometimes I'd stalked their activity for weeks to know when they'd be alone and least expecting it. They wouldn't live to remember their final night, but that didn't mean I couldn't slam so much fear into them that they pissed themselves. Why was I two men? Because I was a little bit crazy. A little bit loco. Life got boring real quick and I was a man who liked to shake things up. I found it all too easy to slip from one person to the other—from barman and charming boss, to stealthy murderer lacking all empathy and remorse.

In this case, my mind was occupied by Harley fucking Davids. I couldn't get her off my mind. I'd tried to talk to Rome this morning, but he was busy. Too busy for me, because his mind was occupied and fixed on something, just like mine was. So tonight I would keep my distance. I wouldn't risk losing a grasp on my control and fucking this up. If there was one thing I was proud of, it was my ability to murder without leaving a shred of evidence, absolutely nothing to lead the police to my door. I killed, I ended, and then I continued until the next time.

I knew my target was out, at some financial event with people who had been born with money, never knew any different, but always screwed the poor fucks of society out of their share of their happiness. They say money can't buy it, happiness, but I knew different. It didn't just pay for contentment; with the right amount of money and just a slither of psychopathy that skewed the needle on the moral compass, money could change everything. Tens of lives in an instant. Money held more money ransom—the more you had, the more you could ruin. I had no doubt Mr Fraser had fucked the wrong man over, lost him a couple of mill that meant his life became worthless, while his death earned a £100,000 price tag.

Letting myself into his apartment, I looked around, trying to find something I could take. *This man*, this persona of mine, liked to keep souvenirs. I liked to keep mementos, pieces of shit that wouldn't show up on an insurance report, but things that I would use as my physical tally— exactly how many kills I had on my non-existent conscience. Mr Fraser was surprisingly modest for a rich prick. His furniture was pretty scarce, his bathroom lacking the collection of colognes and grooming kits I saw as a trend amongst the rich, and his wardrobe was pathetic. Polo shirts hobos wouldn't be seen dead wearing, jeans from the local supermarket, and the dude had a 44-inch waist. With my fingertips protected by the leather gloves I'd pulled on when I got to the front door of his apartment block, I rummaged through his drawers—at least he had Calvin Kleins; he wasn't a complete lost cause. I grabbed a pair of socks from the drawer, picked up a photograph of him next to a model at some car convention, then I shoved them into my pocket and pulled the zip up. I'd chosen my souvenir and I wouldn't risk losing it. The second I'd secured the socks in my pocket, my phone pinged from the breast pocket of my shirt. I pulled it out and glanced at the screen. I allowed myself to smile when I saw the name of the sender. It managed to clear my thoughts and fill my mind with something I hadn't felt since I was a kid. Hope.

> Ariel15: What are you up to? xo
>
> Type Message
>
> **SEND**

Ah, my Ariel. The chick I'd been speaking to for weeks, since I stumbled upon her in a chatroom I used to bounce my communication trail. Her profile image was of the redheaded mermaid from the movie and, you see, I'd always had a thing for redheaded cartoons.

> **Caesar044**: Nothing much. How are you, pretty girl?
>
> **Ariel15**: Wondering how you know I'm a pretty girl. I could be hideous. Maybe that's why you've never seen me 😊 xo
>
> **Caesar044**: You're not hideous. And you haven't seen me either. Perhaps we're too good-looking to be seen together.
>
> **Ariel15**: We'll go with your theory 😊 Will you be on later? xo
>
> **Caesar044**: Maybe. Missing me?
>
> **Ariel15**: Nah. Wondering if I've managed to get rid of you yet xo
>
> *Type Message*
>
> **SEND**

I scoffed a laugh, standing in my target's bedroom, staring down at messages from the only woman who had made no attempt to meet me and let me drag her into bed. She had no interest in me beyond casual conversation and it had become refreshing, less of a challenge and more of an escape where I didn't have to be a boss or a bad guy.

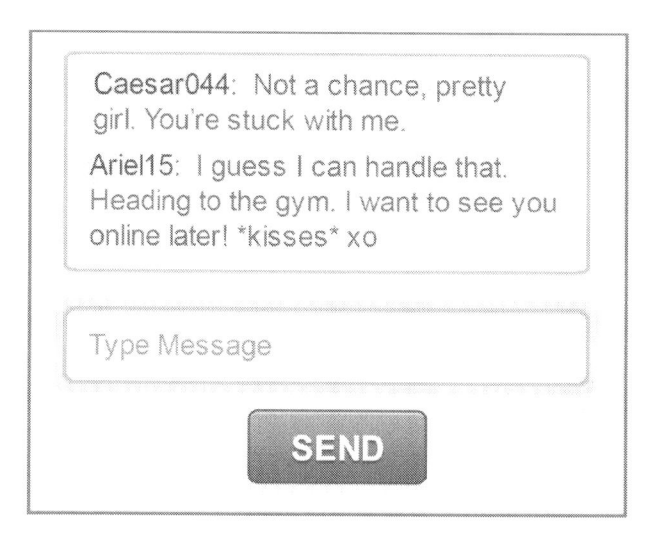

> Caesar044: Not a chance, pretty girl. You're stuck with me.
>
> Ariel15: I guess I can handle that. Heading to the gym. I want to see you online later! *kisses* xo

[Type Message]

SEND

Ariel signed off just in time. When the digits at the top of the screen flicked to 8pm, I knew it was time. Weirdly, I didn't want to be the one to cut her off...I refused to dwell on it right now. I stepped back across the room and hid behind the bedroom door. I wanted to listen to his movements for a while. I let the rush of adrenaline and the premature-satisfaction take me. It was like a high, better than any time I'd smoked a joint or snorted a line of coke—which just turned me into a lunatic, so I didn't do it anymore—and I wanted hit after hit after hit. The ride from every kill got a little duller, until I needed to find something else to intensify the high. I needed to find a way to get back to what I felt the first time. Call it experimentation. Call it indecisiveness. Call it hypocrisy, I didn't give a fuck. I knew what would happen over every one of the next thirty minutes, but I wasn't about to deny myself some fun while it all played out.

Mr Fraser made himself a cup of tea, and I knew he took it with three sugars and a shit-ton of milk. Just the thought of the diabetic coma making its way into his stomach made me realise maybe I'd be putting him out of his misery. Some sort of sugar seizure was no way to go. I'd choose a bullet any day. He sat in his leather wingback with the book he'd been reading over the last few nights; I heard the creak of leather, the flipping of the pages, and the crackle of the fire he'd lit to keep himself warm. I almost felt bad that I'd be stealing him away from such a relaxing evening. Then I smiled…I really wasn't sorry. Neither was the man who had paid me to kill him. When he finished reading, put out the fire and made his way through the hallway towards the bedroom I was still hiding in, I slipped my gun from the waistband of my trousers, unclipped the safety and held it in both hands in front of my legs. I listened to him move around the room from where I hid in the dark corner. He didn't turn a light on and I almost wished he did, so I could smile and yell, *"surprise,"* before shooting him. His trousers hit the floor, sent down by his heavy belt to make a loud thud on the carpet. His shirt was next, whooshing to the floor with a grunt from him. Poor Mr Fraser was tired. How much longer should I make him wait?
3…2…1…

"Good evening, Mr Fraser," I said, stepping out from the shadow.

He jumped, and I saw him pale even in the darkness. He knew. He knew what I was here for, and there was no fear in his eyes.

"It's amazing what money can buy," he whispered, raising his hands and turning to face me as he stepped out of his trousers. "Thank you."

"What?"

"I hired you, Caesar."

"You did what?"

What the fuck? Why would a man hire his own hit? Why hadn't he made more of his last day on Earth instead of spending the evening with boring people talking about boring shit, and then returning home to a boring night alone? And then I remembered...there had been no date on the order. I was just told to kill him, the time and date were up to me, and I realised he *had* ordered his own assassination. He wanted to be surprised, like every other person I'd killed. He was ready for death...why?

"You see, money made me miserable, but I couldn't not spend it. I couldn't not have it. And then I couldn't stop giving it to bad people, for bad things, that made me feel so good. I'm done, boy. I'm asking you to kill me, to save others."

"What the fuck are you on? I should take your money and walk the fuck out." Even as I said the words, I raised the gun and watched him work on a constricted swallow. "No one should order their own hit. How fucking lonely do you have to be?"

"Did you know when you have money you have a world of debauchery at your fingertips? I've fucked underage girls; I've fed them cocaine and injected them with heroin. I've accepted gifts from clients, and they didn't come in gift-wrapped boxes. I don't want to be a bad man..."

I couldn't understand what was going on. All I knew was I wanted to kill him now. *Now* it was personal because he was a fucking idiot. He hadn't been caught. He could have continued to fuck and inject and participate in deviance until he took his last natural breath, but fuck...this guy had a conscience and it had led to him paying to be taken out.

"Shut the fuck up," I spat, taking a step forward to press the barrel of the gun to his forehead. He raised his eyes to look at it, becoming acquainted with the weapon that would end him. I couldn't let him live, even if I wanted to. He'd seen my face. "You really want me to kill you, and spend the money you paid me to do it?"

He nodded.

I shrugged.

"Okay."

I pulled the trigger and the bang echoed around the room as his head flew back, his body followed, and his bedroom was painted a fresh new colour of red, marbled with lumps of his sick brain. Pulling my torch out of my pocket, I shone it around the bedroom as I stepped over his dead body, dodged the bits of him scattered over the carpet, and then I left the room, grabbing a bottle of beer from the fridge in the kitchen before heading out of his apartment with it.

"Good morning, Carter," Peyton said with a smile, glancing over her computer at me as I stopped at her desk.

"Good morning." Leaning on the desk, I smiled at her and edged closer to snag her undivided attention. "How are you?"

"Good, thank you." Her fucking smile got me, causing my dick to stir. Then I noted her eye colour, chocolate fucking brown, and I was transported back to the night I met another. "How are you?"

"Fine. I want to make a donation."

"I figured. I think you singlehandedly keep us going."

"Ah." I swatted my hand through the air. I really didn't want her saying shit like that. I only donated so the taxman didn't take it when I died. "I'm just trying to help."

"Yes, but-"

"Just give me the form," I clipped, growing impatient and needing her to just shut up. She was talking to the wrong man if she expected genuine feelings. "I have things to do."

"Yes, sir." She swivelled in her chair, giving me a glimpse of gossamer sheathed legs made in heaven. I'd been between them and although I wouldn't go again—I didn't double-dip—I would admire the view. "Here you go," she said, handing me the form. "Anonymous?"

"Of course."

I filled in the form, ticking the boxes and leaving all identifiable information blank. Then I reached to the ground and picked up the gym bag I'd brought in with me.

"There's fifty thousand."

"Carter..."

"Seriously, Peyton, it's a drop in the ocean."

"The women will appreciate it."

"I know."

"And their children."

"I know that, too." Shoving the bag towards her, I didn't wait for her to empty it before backing up towards the exit. "I'll be back in a few weeks."

"Thank you." I ignored her, turning and pushing the door open and stepping into the street. "See you soon."

I waved her off over my shoulder and didn't look back before I walked away. I needed to get back to the club and prepare for Saturday night, but I had no urgency to. I knew it was covered. I knew I should take the night off; it was essential to take breaks between kills so talks of a spree and a serial killer on the loose couldn't fall from the lips of people who knew nothing. I didn't just kill innocent civilians. Mr Fraser played on my mind; a rapist, drug-feeding prick who deserved to die, and I refused to let myself feel bad. I wasn't capable of it. Instead, I reminded myself that his death had been worth it, and I felt something...I lacked the experience to label it anything other than *something*, but it was better than nothing. Wasn't it?

"Carter."

I rolled my eyes and stopped walking, remembering I had to be the *nice* guy and keep my unknowing accomplices on my side. I wasn't expecting the object of my newest obsession to be standing in front of me when I turned around.

"Well," I said with a smirk when I took in the sparkle in her eyes that still hinted at a healthy dose of fear. "If it isn't Harley Davids."

"Shouldn't you be off killing people or raping them next to dumpsters?"

"Killing people, huh?" I took a step closer. She was paralysed, curious although frightened. Why had she called me if she had every intention of shying away of whatever it was that passed between us? "Have you been following me?"

She shrugged and a small smile played on her lips then. "I wouldn't waste my energy. I was simply calling you to tell you you're in my way."

"In your way?"

I looked down, and then back up. Damn. Harley was a runner. Why hadn't I noticed that before? Why hadn't I noticed the soft tightness of her abs, the gentle swell of muscular thighs and toned calves that definitely hinted at a competent runner?

"Yeah. You were just standing there in the middle of the street."

"Huh," I scoffed, bemused. I didn't remember stopping. "How many miles have you got left, Farah?"

"Funny." She rolled her eyes. I felt something turn in my stomach and, for once, it wasn't the urge to puke. It was...amusement, perhaps. I wanted to watch her eyes roll again, with me between her legs pumping into her tight cunt. "I'm done, actually. Cooling down on the walk home."

"Great." Taking hold of her shoulder, I smiled when she flinched as I turned her to face the other way, positioning her next to me with my arm around her. It felt...not uncomfortable. "Then let's do coffee."

"How very human of you, Carter," she said, catching my attention with the smart fucking mouth I wanted to fill...and watch as she spoke. "Are you planning on being an asshole?"

"Perhaps." I shrugged. And smiled. She hadn't agreed—yet—but she was walking next to me and we were heading towards the bistro on the corner. "It's who I am, babe."

"Well, then you should know I'm the kind of girl likely to throw coffee all over you if you say something I don't like."

"Well." Dipping lower, I whispered in her ear as I reached for the door handle. "Lucky for you, I like them feisty."

I pushed the door open and let her lead the way.

Because I liked watching her ass as she walked in front of me.

And I didn't trust her not to run off. I wasn't finished with Ms Harley Davids. Far, far from it.

Five
HARLEY

Taking a seat in the window where it seemed safer, I watched Carter stroll to the counter. He was wearing jeans that showcased his firm backside perfectly, and a snug grey t-shirt. His thick hair was styled effortlessly, and as was the case when we first met, he wore that same smug smirk.

He returned with a cup of tea for me and a black coffee for himself, and placed a granola bar in front of me. "Figured you'd need something to lift your energy levels after your run."

I looked at his double chocolate muffin and to the cardboard mush disguised as a 'healthy alternative to chocolate', then reached out, swapping the two around.

He quirked an eyebrow, staring down at the oats and raisin bar. "Do you always take things that don't belong to you, Miss Davids?"

I smirked, tearing into a huge piece of the soft sponge. "Only when they're full of sugar. If you seriously think that a crappy granola bar is going to build my strength then I worry you're living a very boring life, Carter."

He chuckled, tearing the wrapper off the bar with his teeth and taking an experimental bite.

Grimacing, he threw it down and then leaned over and tore a piece of the muffin off.

"On the contrary, I just happen to know that women like to take care of their figures."

Narrowing my eyes, I regarded him. "Are you saying I don't look after my figure?"

A blaze lit his eyes as they dropped to my chest, and then back up to my face. "From where I'm sitting, your figure is maintained to perfection, Harley. Of course, I can't verify that fact until I have seen you naked."

"Then I guess you'll never know."

A smile tilted the corners of his lips, amusement lighting his eyes. "You willing to bet a wager on that, babe?"

Staring at him, I shook my head, and decided not to answer him as I popped the last piece of the cake into my mouth.

His gaze dropped to watch me eat. If he thought I was conscious of him watching me then he would be sorely mistaken.

"So," he muttered as he leaned back and took a sip of his coffee. "I take it your 'business' Saturday night was successful."

I stiffened. Doing my best to appear nonchalant, I took a drink of tea and forced it past the lump in my throat. "What exactly do you want, Carter?"

Holding up his hands, he shook his head. "I'm offended you think I have an ulterior motive. I'm simply asking about your profession."

I wasn't sure if he was serious, or mocking. "You seem like the type of person that has motives for lots of things."

He laughed. "You know me so well already."

"Well enough," I mumbled as I finished my drink and stood up. "Thank you for the drink, and your muffin."

He unashamedly dragged his gaze down my body, his eyes resting on my thighs for a tad too long before sweeping back up to my face. "It was my pleasure." He stood and I started when he rested a hand at the base of my spine, his light touch burning through the thin cotton of my t-shirt, and led me out of the café. "Can I give you a lift anywhere?"

I scoffed. "Are you asking me to climb into a stranger's car, and give him my address? So he can come and murder me in my sleep?"

He chuckled. "Oh, Harley." He leaned into my ear, the rush of his breath over my skin making me shiver. "I already know where you live."

I froze, my eyes widening on him. "What?"

"And I'm quite positive we can find more ways of making you scream than murder."

My belly throbbed, but my heart thundered. "Care to tell me why you find it necessary to stalk me?"

He laughed, the deep rumble making my fists clench. "I am merely taking an interest in your wellbeing. London is far from a safe place, and I'm not sure if I could ever handle someone else making you scream, Miss Davids."

He was infuriating. The flesh of my bottom lip popped when my teeth sunk in too deep and the taste of copper tickled my tongue.

I tensed when Carter lifted a hand and swiped his thumb over the small nick in my lip. He grinned before sliding his thumb between his lips and sucking at the blood. "There is something sweet to you, after all."

"You're a prick." I hissed as I turned and set off into a run, thankful that I was already in my running gear.

"Hey, pricks don't buy pretty girls tea and granola bars. I believe, if I'm sincerely a prick, then you owe me a coffee and a muffin."

Raising my hand above my shoulder, I flipped him off as I continued along the street.

I could feel Carter's gaze on me as he watched me round the corner at the end of the street. I couldn't understand why I reacted the way I did around him. He was an obnoxious arsehole who thought everyone owed him something. He was used to them falling at his feet. Not me. I didn't bow to anyone—anymore. His words from the gallery exhibition last week filtered into my mind.

"Oh, don't worry, I won't take you until you offer it. And believe me, you will offer yourself to me. In fact, I have no doubt that you'll be fucking begging for it."

A smile curved my mouth. The idiot had no idea. It was evident no one had ever turned him down before. Not until me. I couldn't risk allowing Carter to get any closer, to see the real me. He was already too inquisitive, too pushy.

He hadn't quite divulged what he'd witnessed when he'd walked in on me during the job I'd had to finish off for Benny at the gallery, but I had a feeling he'd seen more than I wanted him to. I wasn't sure if he was going to use it to blackmail me, or for some other specific reason, yet I had made sure to completely veil any trace I may have left at the gallery. So unless Carter was a pro, I was certain he had nothing to hold over me.

Spots of rain started to hit my hot skin as I rounded the corner of my street and jogged around the house to the rear steps.

My feet stumbled and I froze on the top step when I saw my back door ajar. The wooden frame was splintered, shards of wood scattered across the porch as the wind that had suddenly got up blew my door further open.

Fishing for my phone out of my bra, I quickly scrolled my contacts and called Evan.

"Harl?"

"I need you. Someone's broken into my house."

The hiss through his teeth made me wince. "Stay outside. I'll be ten."

Carter had a lot to answer for. If this was his idea of letting me know he knew my address, I didn't appreciate his sense of humour.

The door creaked as I pushed it open, the fractured wood breaking even more and sending small chips over my trainers. I tried to calm my racing heart by pressing my palm to my chest as I stepped over the threshold.

"Plum," I called, my eyes hunting for my cat.

Blowing out a breath of relief when she trotted around the corner of the hallway from the kitchen, I scooped her up into my arms and buried my face into her soft grey fur. "Thank God. You okay, baby?" I studied her, my eyes and fingers examining every inch of her to check she wasn't hurt.

Nothing appeared out of place in the hallway and I hesitantly moved into the front room, the pounding of my pulse in my ears too loud as I strived to listen for sounds of an intruder.

But it was quiet. And a complete mess.

My breath hitched when I found the destruction of my home. My sofa had been slashed, the filling spilling out onto the floor. The drawers in my dresser had been pulled free, the contents upended and scattered across the room. Even the carpet had been pulled up and various floorboards uprooted and tossed to the side.

"What the hell?"

Plum meowed and nudged me with her nose when she felt my shock. Tears stung my eyes and I blinked them away, not allowing whoever had done this to control my emotions.

"Jesus."

Evan's voice in the quiet room made me jump and spin around. Plum jumped out of my arms and made a beeline for Evan, her best friend.

"Any idea who did this?" he asked as he picked her up and stroked his hand over her head.

Anger made my chest tight and I clenched my teeth together. "I have a pretty good idea."

"Have you checked the rest of the house?"

I shook my head. He passed Plum back to me then went to inspect upstairs.

The door to the basement was still securely locked; the pin code and finger scan that was required to open it hadn't given the intruder access to what I assumed they'd been looking for. Carter was evidently fucked off that he couldn't get what he needed from the gallery, so he'd tried to find something in my home.

"Upstairs is a mess but nothing that can't be fixed," Evan said as he followed me down the stairs into my office.

The lights switched on as we descended and my equipment fired up, already preparing itself for me.

Evan took a chair to the kit at the back of the room as I logged into the CCTV.

"What is it?" he asked when he heard my sharp intake of breath, and I jolted when his hand squeezed my shoulder.

I turned to look at him and lifted a brow when his eyes widened and fixed on the screen.

"Shit." He stared at the monitor, his face paling slightly. "Is that on a loop?"

"Yep."

He closed his eyes and sighed. "There's only one person we know that could hack into your system, Harl."

His sad gaze on me had me rubbing my hands over my face as I accepted the truth.

Michael was back.

Six
HARLEY

18 Months Ago
"Michael. Oh, Michael."

I rode the high like a nymph...and that's exactly what I was. A dirty fucking nymph—Michael's good little toy.

"You want it, Harley?" he spat, thrusting up into me as I slumped over him. "How badly do you want it?"

"So bad," I slurred, forcing my body to obey my mind and keep me conscious. All I wanted was to slip away. "So, so badly, Michael. I want it so much."

"There's a good little whore," he said with a smack to my arse and a hard thrust that brought his balls up to smack against me. "Make me come, baby."

I grimaced when he pulled out of me, fisted my hair and shoved me to move down the bed. Kneeling between his legs, I took his cock in my mouth, working it with a strong tongue and a hard suck, with an eager hand gripping the base. I sucked him long and hard, the lingering trip to utopia helping his body hold on, hold out, and prologue my payment. He took ages; my gag reflex went into overdrive and my head pounded with the need to get this over with. I needed more. The pulsing in my temples told me to hurry up and claw at my purchase. Exchanging my body for consumables from my sick lover was how I lived my life now. Gone was the girl who attended university with the aspiration to move to Italy, deal in art of the highest quality in a beautiful country—the country of love and romance and hope. I'd hoped Michael and I would do it together but, it wasn't to be...

"Suck it, Harley." He pulled my hair, forcing me to unsheathe my teeth and apply gentle pressure to the tip of his cock. "Suck it, just like Lissy does."

Lissy. My best friend. The blonde-haired, blue-eyed princess who fucked my boyfriend while I was out making coffees and earning the pennies to fund us. Michael thought he was keeping his secret, but I'd known for ages. Of course I'd known; even when I was out of my head, he was inside it. I'd caught them on the sofa last week. She was bent over the back facing the front door they knew I'd walk through. He was behind her, his forearm across her chest as he pounded into her from behind and kept them both facing the door while they waited for me. I wanted to bite his fucking dick off as the memories of them together filled my mind. But then I wouldn't get what I needed.

"Oh, shit." Michael growled and I extended my tongue, opening up for his cum to jet into my mouth. "That's it, my Harley Queen."

Harley Queen. Dumb fuck had no idea it was Harley Quinn, and she was no sweet little woman. Oh, no. She was a villain, she could hold her own, and she fucked the bad guy so good, all the good guys wished they were bad.

Rolling my eyes, I sat up and held out my hand.

"Payment made."

"Oh, baby." He cooed at me. I hated it when he cooed at me like I was a vulnerable infant. I hated it because I played to it. I hated it because every time he called me baby, I nuzzled into his hand, purred like a damn cat and wished he'd hold me and tell me he loved me. "Don't be in such a hurry."

I was in a hurry. I was in a massive hurry. I could hear my heart beating in my ears and the rapid heavy flurry had nothing to do with the orgasm I'd just faked. My hands were shaking, sweat pooled at the bottom of my neck, across my forehead and down my temples, and my eyes darted from side to side. I knew the effects of going so long were beginning to take over and I needed to make them go away. I needed to numb the pain and forget who I was again. I could never go back to remembering because then I would remember I had failed and Daddy had told me it was never okay to fail. But that was before he'd failed for the last time and the man with the leather gloves came for him.

"Here you go, darling," he muttered. "Make the memories go away."

See, at times like this, Michael was my hero. He knew what I needed. He'd always known what I needed. He'd been there during my first year of university, and he'd been there the day my parents died. He'd walked me home from campus, I'd waved him goodbye at the door knowing he was going to rugby training and I'd see him later...five minutes later, I was an orphan, having watched the murderer flee the scene with nothing more than a bloody glove sliding around the doorframe before he escaped out of the back door. I began shaking, remembering the blood. The bodies of my mother, father and baby brother laid out on the living room floor like a barcode, complete with white sheets between the black ones they were wrapped in.

"Harley..." Michael dragged me back from the day I'd lost everything, and tossed the little clear packet onto my lap. "Take it and come back to bed."

He pulled the bedsheet up to over his softening cock and turned onto his side to pour the delicate white powder out in a thin line. I licked my lips, salivating as he took the rolled up note he'd used earlier and snorted the cocaine. Swallowing hard, I squeezed the bag in my fist and crawled up the bed to the cabinet on the side where I slept. Michael's hot hands caressed my bare back as I set up my own line, and he dragged the twenty-pound note up over the crack of my arse, along my spine and over my shoulder into my waiting hand. I wasn't ashamed when I leaned lower—face down, arse up was the best way to be, he said—*and took a sharp draw in, feeling the powdery substance fill my nostril, leaving a numbing trail down the back of my throat as it made its way to my head and into my blood.*

"That's my girl," Michael said, dragging my languid body to lie on my back next to him. I saw him squeeze my breast, but I was unaware of everything else he did as I allowed my mind to float away on a cloud. "Switch it all off, baby."

Switch it off.

I nodded, letting my eyes roll back as he pulled the sheet up over my legs and then over his head. He moved lower, parting my legs and reminding me exactly why I complied to his demands.

Present Day

"Have you called the old bill?" Benny asked, walking in with a cardboard holder filled with coffee cups. Cappuccinos for us, and a small warm milk for Plum.

"Absolutely not," I said, taking a cup out of the holder and trying to force a smile for him.

I knew Benny would blame himself. I knew he would think it was his fault Michael had been able to get back into my life but, the truth was, he would always have a way, because he had my life on a key around his neck. He'd used Benny, exploited his lack of expertise and I'd played right into his hands. The rest had been easy.

"Why not?"

"Ben-" Evan warned, taking his own coffee and taking the lid off Plum's.

"It's okay," I said. "The police can't help me here. Sure, they'll open up a case and investigate a home invasion, but nothing was taken. And you really think the police would just take a glance over my kit and shrug it off?"

"So why did he come in if..." The constant smile Ben always wore dropped and his deep green eyes filled with fear. For me. It was something I wasn't used to, and something I refused to feel for myself. "He left something behind."

"Yes."

"And you can't show the police."

"No."

"So it's not the kind of gift you had on your Christmas list."

"Bingo!" I clicked my fingers and gave him a jazz hands. Anything to bring that smile back. "Seriously, it's fine. A little cleaning up and life goes on."

"He's done this before," Evan said. "He likes her to know he's still alive."

"Unfortunately," the three of us said together.

Smiling, I shook my head and took a step back.

"Listen, I need five minutes, okay? Can I leave you to finish tidying up here? I just want to check some stuff downstairs."

"Sure thing," Evan said. "We'll sort out a more secure front door, too."

"Thank you."

I left them to it, letting myself into the basement and locking the door behind me. He'd gotten in. I thought I'd taken all the necessary precautions to keep him out of my life like I couldn't do my mind, but Michael had gotten in. It didn't terrify me that he'd broken into my house. If he was going to hurt me, he could do it without taunting me first. It didn't terrify me that he'd torn my house apart; I didn't care that he'd taken my knickers out of the drawers and scattered them around the house; I didn't care that he'd taken the last bottle of beer from the fridge, and I didn't care that he'd ruined my furniture. No...what terrified me was what he'd preserved. What he'd kept damage and erosion-free. He'd been in my workplace and he could have ruined it. But he didn't.

Nor had he allowed time to heal his obsession the way time hadn't healed the addiction.

The sound of my own heavy breathing filled the room as I looked at the screen and saw an emaciated twenty-four-year-old woman begging to be left alive.

It was the day I'd paid for my last hit...

12 months ago

"Harley, my queen." I opened my eyes and saw Michael through the fog. "I'm in a bit of trouble."

"Are you?" I scrubbed my eyes with the heels of my hands and sat up, allowing the sheet covering me to flutter to my lap. "What's wrong?"

"She'll do," a low voice boomed across the room, making me jump.

When I looked towards the door, I gasped. Three men stood in the doorway, filling it entirely until there was no hope for natural light and very little hope for me. I looked at the window. Michael had all but blocked us in entirely; he'd got angry with me a few months ago and put his fist through the window so he wouldn't put it through me. He'd boarded most of it up and had promised to replace it, but there were more important things to pay for.

"You're a pretty young thing." The man at the front of the pack stalked toward me, stroking his

chin. "When Mikey here told me he would offer his missus up, I expected a crater-face crack whore." He narrowed his eyes at me and dipped lower to get a good look. "If I'm not mistaken, I'd say you even have all your teeth."

"Fuck you," I spat, scratching my nails up over my forearm. "What do you want?"

"Sorry, Harley." Michael shrugged and slinked off the bed, falling back to stand in the corner.

"Lover boy didn't tell you?" the big—biggest—guy asked.

I shook my head.

The other two laughed. What was going on?

"You see," the second guy started, walking into the room, followed by the third giant until they surrounded me and I curled up tightly on the bed with my back to the headboard. "Mikey here is in a bit of debt."

"A lot of debt." The third guy laughed. "He thought he could run. He thought he could go out of town to score and then waltz back in here like he didn't owe us."

"I'm sorry," I whispered, my bottom lip trembling as the leader sat on the end of the bed and Michael folded his arms across his chest. "How much does he owe you? We can figure something out."

He tipped his head to the side, his gaze taking in my features. I tried to look sober. What would happen if he realised I took his drugs, too?

"Did he ease you into it?" he asked, reaching out and swiping his finger under my nose, ignoring my

wince and the squeal that left me. "Did he tell you it would make it all better if you took just a little bit?"

I paused, looked away, then looked at Michael before I nodded.

"You see, that means you were pretty weak. Daddy issues?" He shook his head. "Nah, you're far too shy to have been abused by Daddy. So it's...neglect? Ah-" He smirked before clicking his fingers and pointing at me. "Orphaned."

I cried, realising I couldn't stay strong by asking this man and his minions to feed my habit. A habit Michael had forced on me when he could no longer cope with consoling a grieving girlfriend.

"Insensitive prick, isn't he?" the second guy asked, placing his hand on my shoulder. I froze. "I mean, if he'd have just spent a few more nights rocking you to sleep, you'd be sober now, probably in a post-grad job and living in one of those posh pads in the city."

"Instead you're here," the third guy retorted, moving around the bed to sit on the other side. "About to pay for your boyfriend's coke habit. Dirty stuff, cocaine. Rots you from the inside out. First your mind." He stabbed his finger to my temple.

"Then your nose." The second guy reared forward, pinching my nose as his palm covered my mouth.

"Then your body."

The leader punched me in the stomach. I screeched, my ears popping as I tried to expel air from my lungs to aid a scream. He grabbed my ankles and jolted me to lie back on the bed, as the second and third man stood and loomed over me.

Michael said nothing.
He said nothing.

Seven
HARLEY

I had made many mistakes over the twelve months since Michael used me to pay for his drug debt, and pissing off his dealers. The biggest mistake was the one I made over and over again; I thought I was over him and the ordeal he'd forced me through. I proved myself wrong time and time again—every time I reached for a little white pouch of powder and told myself I was *deciding* to do this. I refused to acknowledge my addiction which meant one thing…I was never going to get better. I refused to admit I had a problem, which meant the cycle continued as the months passed.

But today, I felt better. Somewhere deep in my mind I knew it would only be a matter of time before I proved myself wrong again, but I didn't care. Michael had returned to my life in more than just a cocaine-induced haze; he'd broken into my home, worked his way beyond my defences without so much as a breadcrumb left behind. And yet, I felt calm. I hadn't contacted my dealer last night; I hadn't crawled into my bed and prayed I'd never wake. No. I watched the footage he'd planted on my system; it played in a loop and I watched every single time, until Evan came to get me, insisted I showered and ate something, and then we got back to work.

I wasn't going to let Michael get away with what he'd done to me. I was Frank Davids' daughter; there was only a handful of people on the planet who knew the real Frank and, not only had I inherited his blood and last name, I'd inherited his ruthlessness. His hunger for justice. His ability to seek revenge without hesitation. After my family's murder, I'd plummeted into grief and a full two years of mourning meant Michael became my solace. I'd been vulnerable, susceptible to his subconscious abuse, and I'd fallen victim to the power of white powder. It had taken the three men who beat me, abused me, and spent two days raping me, waking me when I passed out just to take me again and again, to bring me to life. I'd stepped out of the cloud of mourning I used as an excuse to be a victim, and I decided I'd honour my father by taking revenge for his death...but first, Michael.

And Carter. I wouldn't, and couldn't, deny that he was part of the reason for the latest phase of recovery. I hated him. I knew nothing about him—nothing except that he was a crude, secretive snake—but I needed to be of sane mind around the clock. He'd popped up unannounced twice, and while I felt like he had a motive for bursting into my life, I needed to be alert every time he showed up. I needed to figure out what he wanted from me, so I could deny him, shut him down and wave goodbye with a grin as he walked out of my life defeated.

"I have a runner!" Evan exclaimed with a laugh as the sound of his fingers on the keys sped up, his stern glare on the monitor a stark contrast to the humour in his voice. "Coward!"

I snapped out of my trance, glancing at my screen to see I'd managed to multitask—simultaneously breaking my way into the securest platform in the country, and thinking about last night...and my lack of pain in the aftermath.

I sighed, shaking my head as my fingers moved over my own keyboard as my eyes fixed hard on Evan's monitor. "Stop playing with your food, Evan."

He laughed louder, throwing his head back in sheer amusement, as Ben came to stand behind him, excitement making him bounce around on the balls of his feet. Ben was always so full of energy that Evan and I were jealous of him. I couldn't function without at least six cups of coffee and a few smokes in the morning, yet Ben was one of those annoying people that woke up whistling. The three of us made a great team; Ben was the charismatic little pup, Evan was the sensible brother-figure that kept us both in line, and I was the ticking time bomb who relied on them both to survive some days.

I squinted from across the room as I watched various encryptions stream down the black screen. I smiled when Evan continued to cheer in delight at the amateur ciphers, as he sent back a virus within seconds of him instantly creating it. Evan was the virus expert of the team. He could write and program infected packages off the top of his head that specifically catered to whomever, or whatever, we were up against. "Who the fuck is this idiot?"

I turned back to my own screen, leaving the adolescent boys to play. I was glad of their current distraction and once again, for the hundredth time, my patience quickly died when I was kicked back out. I wouldn't give up trying to hack into the database I needed. The beat of my heart paused and the breath in my lungs froze when suddenly, miraculously, 'Access granted. Welcome to the National Security Database, Agent McCuskey' glared in bright green letters on my screen. *Thank you, Agent McCuskey, whoever you are, for selecting such an easy passcode.*

Inputting numerous names, features, known associates and specific crimes, I entered all the info I already had, and I prayed as the software did its work. Various names and photographs flashed at lightning speed until it suddenly stopped on one particular file.

My heart began to gallop. My mouth dried and my lungs bucked in shock when I couldn't pull in any air. My teeth trembled both in hatred and grief, and my hands shook as I moved the cursor and clicked to open the file.

I couldn't stop staring at the photograph, his leer bringing back memories that were suddenly too painful, inhibiting my rapid movements on the keys. Each scar on my body tingled in awareness as my mind screamed in horror.

"Harl?"

I jumped when Evan and Ben loomed over me from behind, both their stares narrow and suspecting. Evan looked from the screen to me, and he tipped his head. "Is this one of them?"

I nodded slowly, my wet eyes fixed to my friend's angry ones. "Number One."

They both looked at me, and nodded. "Time to begin."

"Time to begin," I echoed quietly.

Eight
CARTER

I hadn't heard from her in days, and as if she suddenly sensed me thinking about her, my private, and very secure, IM lit up.

> **Ariel15:** Hey, are you there?
>
> Type Message
>
> **SEND**

It hadn't escaped my notice that she hadn't ended the message with her usual hugs and kisses, and I sat upright, sensing her seriousness. I wouldn't deny, I'd been enjoying the banter that bounced back and forth between us most days. Nor would I deny that I knew she wanted something from me. We'd talked about it, before we'd slipped into an odd online relationship that involved talking about what was for dinner, what she'd done at the gym, and what our plans were for the weekend. All lies on my end, of course, but I still allowed myself to enjoy her virtual company. But her message brought me crashing down to Earth and reminded me why I was the man I was. I typed out a quick reply, trying to maintain the casualness of our friendship, while wanting to scream at her to identify herself so I could punish her one-tracked mind. Women were master manipulators, but I'd figured Ariel out right off the bat.

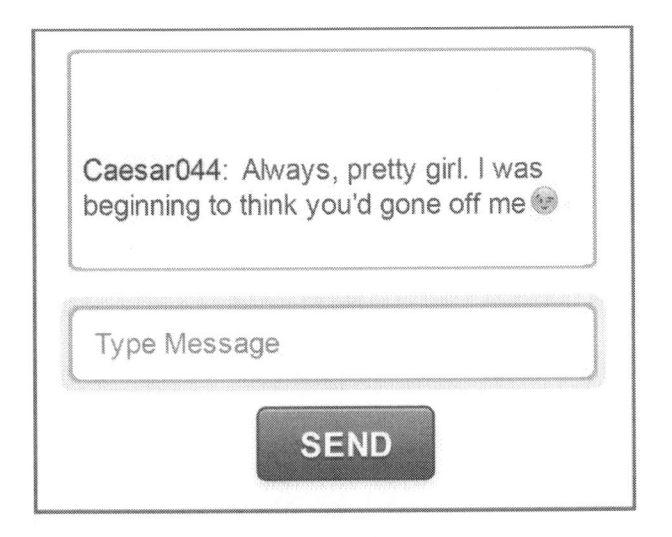

> Caesar044: Always, pretty girl. I was beginning to think you'd gone off me 😊

There was a pause in her reply and the hairs on the back of my neck rippled in preparation. Part of me hoped she was lonely and just wanted to talk, but the realistic part of me—the part I listened to above all others—told me everything.

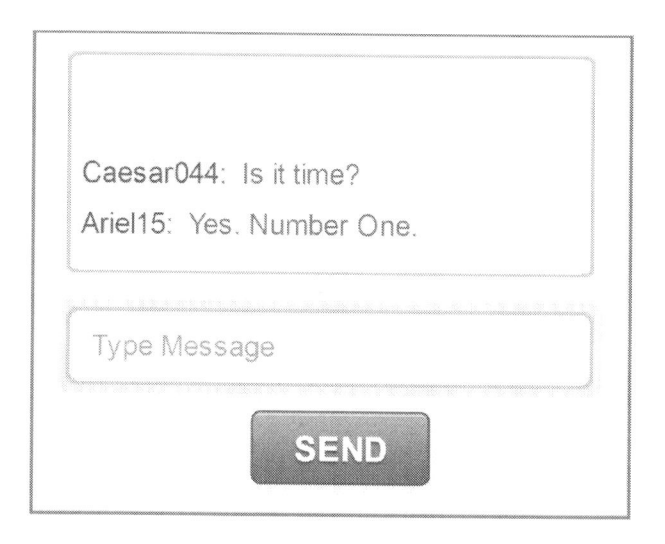

> Caesar044: Is it time?
> Ariel15: Yes. Number One.
>
> Type Message
>
> **SEND**

A swell of excitement and admiration ran through my veins. Excitement? Admiration? It was a first—the first time I'd felt anything but emptiness at what I knew was about to happen. I crossed the apartment to grab a bottle of beer as I typed out a reply. I wasn't unaware at how strange this was. How casual it was, when it should have been anything but. I was acutely aware that we both had our wires crossed. Perhaps that was why we connected the way we had. *No, Carter.*

> **Caesar044**: Clever girl. I'm proud of you. Didn't think you'd follow through.
> **Ariel15**: Of course. I shouldn't, but I trust you. Tell me I'm not making a mistake.
> **Caesar044**: You can trust me. I've told you that. You needn't be nervous. If this is what you want, I'll take it from here.
> **Ariel15**: Will you forward the necessary?
> **Caesar044**: Of course. You know where to send the file, pretty girl.

Type Message

SEND

I was tempted to do it for free. There was something about Ariel that reached out to me, no matter how much I tried to push it away. I couldn't figure it out, but I knew that Number One on her list of four was important to her. I knew this fucker had hurt her; for that very reason I wanted to rip his balls off and drop them at Ariel's feet. I'd already decided to give her a discount, and I would explain it away as a 'buy three get one free.' I couldn't help but smile at my own humour.

My email pinged almost immediately, and I quickly opened it, needing to see this motherfucker. He was an ugly shit, and the blood in my veins started to boil with need as I stared at his photograph.

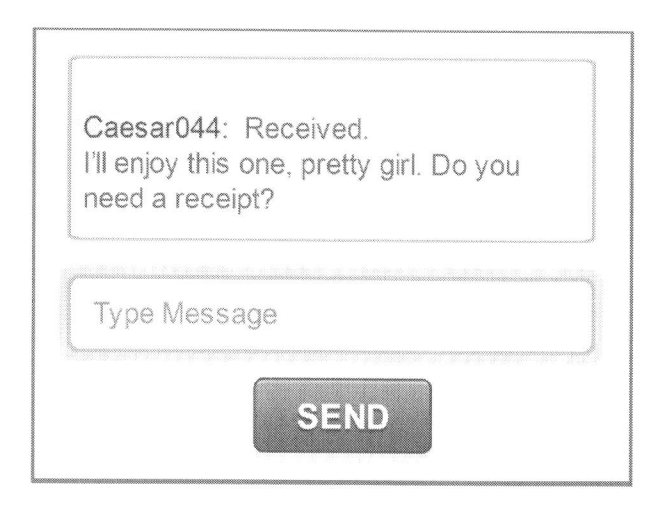

> Caesar044: Received. I'll enjoy this one, pretty girl. Do you need a receipt?

[Type Message]

SEND

She knew that *receipt* meant photographic evidence of job done. I was eager to see whether or not she would accept, and when her confirmation came through, my dick shot to life, excitement at her thirst for blood and retribution calling out to me. Maybe there was hope yet. I had a feeling Ariel's air of hunger for deviance extended further than hiring a hitman, and I wanted to explore just how far I could push it.

> Ariel15: Yes.
>
> Type Message
>
> SEND

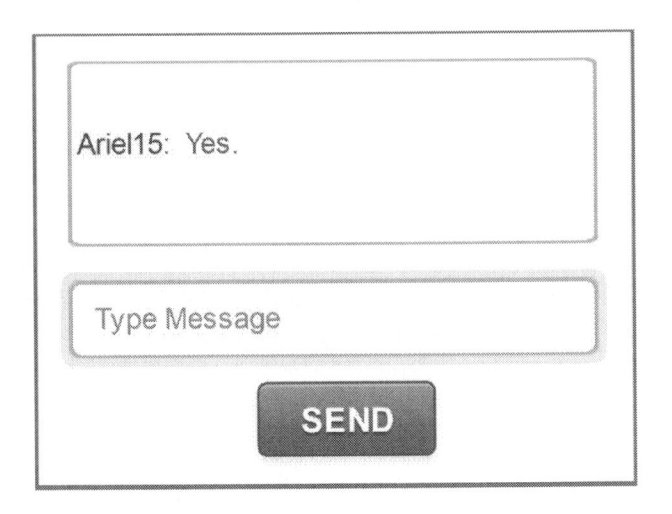

She terminated the chat as I memorised the specific details and burnt the file.

Jobe smirked at me when I turned in the chair and grinned. "Time to play?"

"Hard," I confirmed. "Very hard."

Revealing the email trail, I bounced it around a bit and hid it in some unsuspecting fuck's inbox. There was no evidence it had ever been through my multiple servers, altered IP addresses and in my hands as an attachment on my phone.

Every job I did catered to the lust that lived inside me. I always made sure to do a thorough job. Except this time, it felt personal. Thorough wouldn't be enough for Ariel. I wanted to rip this prick apart until there was nothing left but skin and bone. I wanted to reduce him to dust, so not even Hell would accept him.

Jack Forbes hung before me. Half of his skin decorated the floor beneath him, each slither curling like dried peel across the plastic sheeting spread out to catch any 'bits'. No teeth remained in his mouth, each one lined up perfectly on the hostess trolley Jobe always liked to fill with various 'tools'. The bottom shelf was always littered with numerous body parts. The sick bastard also liked to fill one of the trays housed in the top shelf with goddam peanut M&Ms, frequently popping them into his mouth as he worked beside me.

I guessed Jack would have narrowed his eyes with hatred—well he might have, if he wasn't missing both eyelids. "You're going to die, you sick fucks!" he spat, blood spraying over my 'work clothes' with every venomous word.

Jobe grinned, slipping a yellow M&M into his mouth and crunching on it noisily. "Funny one, this one," he laughed as he picked up a bodkin and a hammer. I cringed at the glee that sizzled in his eyes as he turned up the music and dropped to a crouch before Jack.

Jack squealed when Jobe carefully lined up the tip of the bodkin under his big toenail and hit the hammer.

"Fuck!" he screamed. I smiled. I knew what was coming. "Just tell me what you want and I'll give it you. Anything!"

I inhaled deeply. "We don't want anything, mate. Just to hurt you."

"Why?" he sobbed, his chest heaving with the immense amount of pain he was in. It was inspiring to watch how much a human could withstand before their brain gave in and plunged them into unconsciousness. Jack was particularly withstanding, which surprised me. Although, he had been so high on crack when we'd picked him up that I suspected some of it was still streamlining his veins and giving the motherfucker a little relief.

His chin dropped to his chest. Finally.

Jobe slapped him hard, bringing him back round. "Not yet, crater face."

"Why won't you just kill me and be done with it?"

He stared up at me when I snapped another photo of him, his red-rimmed, lidless eyes making him look comical. "Why the fuck do you keep taking photos?"

"My client wants to watch each moment of your death."

"Your client?" He spluttered on the blood that ran down the back of his throat. "Who the fuck is your client?"

"Hmm," I murmured, dropping to my haunches before him. "Well, see, I was hoping you'd be able to help me with that."

Jobe frowned at me. We never wanted to know any details about clients. Yet, Ariel intrigued me. I couldn't understand why, but I wanted to know everything about her. I needed to know who she was, and I knew Jobe would understand when I let him in.

I slapped Jack's cheek when he started to drift away. "Come on, sunshine. Give me a clue who'd want you dead."

He tried to shake his head, but it drooped again. This was the best part. Sometimes assassination didn't call for quick death with a bullet between the eyes. Sometimes it called for...*more*. We had to take some pleasure from it, right? We deserved to enjoy our job, didn't we?

Grabbing his hair, I yanked his head back. "You're one of four, does that help?"

His head shook and I had to grip onto him harder to keep it from falling back again.

"A woman hired me."

Something, recognition, flashed in his eyes and a slow grin curved across his massacred face. I knew I would slice his fucking lips off next, so he couldn't ever smile again. "Ahh, Mikey's girl."

"Mikey's girl?"

"Who'd have thought the bitch had it in her." His words were slurred and slow as the life in his eyes slowly started to die out.

"Who – is – Mikey's – girl?" I shook him. "Give me a name!"

"What the fuck?" Jobe hissed, his hard accusing eyes glaring at me. "Why are you doing this?"

"You'll see."

My control began to wane when Jack started to drift away. His mouth opened and as his last breath left him, a name made the air in my lungs congeal. "Harley Davids."

Nine
HARLEY

The place was heaving, my fear of enclosed places making my blood heat with need as soon as we stepped foot inside.

"Give it a chance," Ben coaxed with a small smile as he took my hand and guided me through the throng of people and over to the bar.

Dance music made the club seem to physically throb. The stench of sweat and alcohol clung heavily in the air as my feet stuck to the residue on the floor, my shoes slipping off my feet with every step. The strobe lights made my eyes ache, and the thrum of excitement made my head buzz.

I just wanted to go home.

Ben leaned over the bar ordering drinks, as I took a look around the club. Benny had wanted to bring me for a while, but I'd always refused. Yet yesterday's breakthrough saw me following my friends for a celebratory night out. Was it sick that I wanted to celebrate the gruesome death of someone?

A part deep down inside me simmered with a hint of repulsion, however, every single scar Jack Forbes had left on me itched with fulfilment. The clog of fear and revulsion in my lungs was freed—just a fraction—with each breath I had taken since Caesar had forwarded the pictures. Most had turned my stomach, bile scorching my throat with each sickening shot. But I hadn't been able to look away, the depraved part that lived inside me dancing with pleasure at the evident torture the man I'd hired had put him through. For me.

Evan gestured for me to follow him to a booth in the corner away from the pit of dancing bodies.

Blowing out a relieved breath at the open space, I finally smiled and took a sip of my beer.

"I can't believe you've never been here before, Harl," Benny shouted in my ear over the thud of some techno shit.

Just shrugging, I took another drink, the need for oblivion making me draw harder and greedier. Evan watched me with narrow, knowing eyes. "Maybe you should get laid instead," he offered, studying the vicinity with a serious expression.

Beer splattered the table when I choked. "I can't believe you said that!"

"Well, come on. You never go out, you never fuck. You need a life, Harl."

"I do have a life!" I argued. "The gallery and you guys are my life."

Rolling his eyes, Benny leaned forward, joining in the 'gang up on Harley' discussion. "But there's nothing better at relieving tension than a good fuck."

I sighed, shaking my head. "Then I'll buy a vibrator. I don't need a man in my life. I don't *want* a man."

"Who said anything about having a man in your life? I was talking about a fuck, Harley, not a relationship. We don't need a hanger-on. We're greedy and we're keeping you to ourselves..."

"Doesn't mean you can't bang a dude 'til the cows come home and send him on his way after receiving some fresh milk."

"Ew." Heat exploded across my cheeks and I smacked them both in the chest. "It's not that easy for me, you know it isn't."

Once again, Benny rolled his eyes at my anxieties. "It's all in your head."

"It's all over my fucking body!" I hissed, losing my patience with his lack of understanding.

Scowling at me, Evan lowered his voice. "There's only you that sees your scars for what they are. Any guy would be fucking lucky if you paid them the slightest bit of attention."

"Yeah," I murmured, giving up on the argument. They would never understand. And if I was honest, they loved me for who I was, their best friend. I wasn't their lover, so they couldn't comprehend my fear. Sometimes, I did wonder if they were right, that a one-time fuck could be a way out for me, but then my mind would send an image of my mutilated body into my head and remind me just how fucking repulsive I was.

"Let's dance," Benny suddenly declared when he sensed my sombreness and tugged on my hand, pulling me free of the booth before I could refuse.

Benny had moves that a damn choreographer would be jealous of. I couldn't figure out if it was because he was gay, or just that he had an agility that made his frame move fluidly. He was tall and slim, not an ounce of fat on his body that would hinder the rhythm he clearly had. I, however, had a more curves than a Spirograph, and that meant all I was capable of was provocative gyration that would only attract the wrong attention.

His hands slipped over my hips as he pulled me back against him, my back to his front as a tune we both loved blasted from the huge speakers around the room.

"Sorry," he mumbled in my ear.

Looking over my shoulder, I smiled and shook my head. "Nothing to be sorry for. You love me, and I know you're trying to help."

Dropping a kiss to the tip of my nose, he returned my smile, his love for me reflected through his eyes. "I do love you, and I worry about you, sweetheart. That's all it is."

"I know."

"No more shit," he declared, swinging his hips and directing my own with his hands. "Time to set yourself free. Be happy. One down, three to go."

Three to go. Three more deaths until my nightmares were massacred along with the pain that forever lived inside me. Three more deaths until I had promised myself no more Cloud.

Sweat made my hair stick to my face. Heat made my skin burn, and exhaustion had me panting as I approached the bar to replenish our drinks. Although I had been reluctant to party with my friends, I had to admit that I'd had a brilliant night. I hadn't been brave enough to flirt back with any guys who had shown me attention, but Evan and Ben had been understanding and allowed me just to take the night at my own pace.

Digging out my purse from my bag, I looked up when the barman asked what I wanted. Surprise made my eyes widen when one green and one blue eye stared back at me. My mouth popped open in shock and the order of drinks in my head evaporated.

Carter stared at me expectantly. Recognition didn't flash in his eyes and I frowned. "For once you seem lost for words, Carter."

He blinked, then squinted, before awareness finally filtered in. "Harley Davids."

I shouldn't have been as hurt as I was that he didn't instantly recognise me, and I rolled my eyes as I dug into my purse. "I'm so thrilled you remembered."

He smirked at the sarcasm in my voice, and tipped his head. "Well someone seems a little upset. Have you been thinking of me, babe?"

"Grow up."

He leaned forward, a grin slowly curving the edges of his plump lips. "I've been thinking of you. Of that hot little body squirming beneath me, your exquisite little moans in my ear. My name screaming from you when I fuck you into oblivion and make you come hard over my cock."

Heat poured over my skin and into my belly, his crudeness making my body suddenly aware. For a long moment I couldn't speak and I stood gawping at him.

His chuckle brought me round and I clenched my teeth together. "Fuck you."

"Exactly," he mocked as I about turned and made my way back to the boys.

Fingers wrapped around my wrist and I was suddenly spun around, my body colliding with a firm chest. His touch on my skin sent a current up my arm and I shivered.

"Not so fast…" he breathed in my ear, "I thought you wanted a drink."

He was warm; his body heat was so high, I expected a fever, but when my eyes met his it was lust I saw boring into me. His eyes travelled down the length of my body, our closeness showing him the red silk of my bra peeking out from behind the shoulder strap of my dress.

"Red underwear, babe?" he asked, reaching between us to ping the garment. "Have I told you red is my favourite colour?"

I stared up at him, the few inches he had on me making my neck crane. The heat stole me next; my core throbbed as the red knickers that matched my bra saturated with arousal. I couldn't speak. Not a single word would pass my lips, and I knew if I opened my mouth a needy moan would escape.

"What's the matter?" he asked with a smirk. "Cat got your tongue?"

I nodded. Then I shook my head. What was wrong with me? The alcohol swam in my veins and travelled to my mind, making us swirl in the centre of the club. I reached up and gripped his arms.

"Carter…"

My voice was hoarse and seductive, an unintentional rasp taking over. I had no control. I was always in control. How had he stolen it so easily?

"Oh, she speaks," he said, running his finger over my bottom lip. "How would you like to say my name again when you're in my bed?"

I shook my head. Then I nodded. What was going on? Carter's hand slithered down my body, down the side of my waist before he took my hand and threaded his fingers between mine. His free hand cupped my cheek, keeping my hair out of my face as he leaned closer. I didn't think Carter No-last-name, or No-first-name Carter would be capable of softness, but when his full lips brushed mine there was nothing but a warm sensuality that promised so much more.

Evan and Ben's words rang in my mind and I thought, perhaps, Carter was the one. Not The One, the one, but the one who would give me what I needed. A quick one night fuck and a cab ride home in the morning. Carter didn't seem like one for relationships, and I wasn't either. Maybe we'd be a match made in one-night-stand heaven.

"Harley?" he whispered against my lips.

I realised I'd stopped kissing him. My lips were unmoving against his, but they were wet. He'd tried to sneak his tongue past them, but I'd zoned out wondering if I could do this.

"Let's take this somewhere else," I whispered, raising my hand to give his hand a gentle tug. "I'm not one for public displays of…"

"I'm not one for affection, babe."

"Luckily for you, that's the last thing I want."

"Where are your friends?"

"They'll understand."

"Will they?"

"They told me to find a man to fuck."

His chuckle was low and throaty. He didn't need to raise his voice over the music. I heard him clearly, like a blind man saw the world around him without looking.

"Did they now?" I nodded. "And they'd approve of me?"

"I don't give a fuck," I snapped, feeling the edge of alcohol begin to wear. "Are we doing this or not?"

"Are you prepared to beg?"

"Like hell I am."

With a final smirk, Carter stepped back, keeping my hand held tightly in his, and led me round to the opening of the bar. Taking two shot glasses from the cabinet, he poured us both a bright yellow liquor and held the glass to my lips.

"Open."

I did, allowing him to tip the alcohol into my mouth. It instantly slipped down my throat, the burning lemon more than welcome.

"Limoncello?" I asked, licking my lips to catch every drop.

"It tastes good and does the job."

I giggled, feeling giddy from more than the alcohol as I watch him drink his.

"There have been many she's, Harley. If an affectionless fuck is what you're after, I'm your man. I can't promise you'll have had your fill after one night, though."

"Try me."

With a growl, Carter stole me from the club, dragging me through the crowd with ease as it parted like the Red Sea. My anxiety was gone. My fear was gone. My worries were gone. I was completely and utterly consumed by this man and I didn't want reality to find me.

Ten
HARLEY

Carter's apartment was impressive. Even through the drunken haze I noted the starkness of his home. White everywhere. Chrome and black made it feel sterile and I kicked my shoes off the second he stepped inside.

"I'm a neat-freak," he said, noting my action. "Sometimes."

Sometimes? I was sure neat-freaks were neat-freaks every day of the week. I shrugged, crossing the space without his permission until my bare feet found a thick grey rug with silver threads. I squished my toes and smiled.

"Why are you smiling?" he asked as his hands cupped my shoulders. "I wouldn't be smiling if I were you."

"Why not?" I turned to face him. "You think I'm afraid of you?"

"Maybe you should be."

"Because maybe you're a serial killer, or a rapist, or something equally as heinous?" When he said nothing, I reached forward and opened the first button on his shirt. "I wouldn't be afraid if you were."

"No?" One eyebrow, the one above his blue eye, quirked and he looked down at me with curiosity. "Why's that?"

"Because I'm more than aware that monsters don't hide under the bed and wait until you're ready. I've met enough monsters to become desensitised to the danger."

I clamped my mouth shut, snagging both lips between my teeth to stop anymore bullshit escaping.

"Time to stop talking, Harley."

I nodded, grateful for the instruction. He didn't want to hear any more, and I didn't want to say any more. We'd both be satisfied if I kept my mouth shut and-

I jumped him. Wrapping my arms around his neck, I fused my lips to his, desperate to taste him like he'd tried to allow me to downstairs. When he growled and parted his lips, his firm tongue slipping into my mouth, I moaned. Squeezing my ass, he pulled me tight against him and slinked his hands into my hair.

"I need you to beg, Harley," he said, edging me back against the floor to ceiling window that exposed the city and invited its visitors to watch us.

"I don't beg," I said, remembering a time not so long ago when I'd begged for my life.

"I can make you."

"You can't."

"Challenge accepted."

I shrieked when he forced his hands beneath my dress and tore at my underwear. I didn't care when he stuffed them in his pocket. I didn't care when he shoved the dress up higher and managed to tangle my arms in it to hold me captive. I did, however, care when he dropped to his knees and thrust his face between my legs. I quivered when he took a deep breath.

"You smell like a queen," he said. "Like the queen of the villains."

Visions of a woman dressed like a harlequin with pigtails dyed pink and blue tried to steal me from the moment, but Carter took me right back when he threw one of my legs over his shoulder and closed his mouth over my pussy.

"Such a sweet little cunt," he mused with a gentle lick that made me mewl. "All mine...for one night only?"

"Yes," I moaned.

"And you won't beg me? Just once?"

Shaking my head, I whispered, "No."

"Then you've sealed the deal for a second night." A finger slid between my lips and sunk into my pussy. I threw my head back against the glass. "We'll have to go again and again and again until you beg."

"Why?" I asked, fisting his hair and riding his hand to rub my clit against his palm. "Why do you need me to beg?"

"Because we both like to win, babe. I win when you beg, and you win because you'll get rid of me."

I wanted to beg, not because I was prepared to give in, but because I needed some relief. My body was coiled up tight and I needed him to set me free.

"Carter..."

"Don't do it now," he whispered, swirling his tongue over my clit as a second finger eased inside me. "Don't let me win so easily."

"You're a bastard."

"Better believe it, babe." Looking up at me, he shook his head from side to side, stimulating every one of my senses until I shook with an impending orgasm. "Now…do you want it against the wall, or in my bed?"

"Bed."

Before I could explain myself, or think the decision through, Carter stood and hoisted me up to wrap my legs around him. He walked me through the apartment with his lips on mine and his mouth devouring me. I could taste myself on his tongue and I ground against him when his hard cock barely contained by his trousers nudged against my bare pussy.

I landed on the bed with a muted thud as Carter crawled over me and dragged my dress up to expose me to him. I stopped him before he could expose my breasts and he looked at me questionably.

"You can see the only part you'll need," I said, battling against him as he tried to take the dress off. "Take your clothes off and fuck me already."

"If that's how you want to play it."

Leaning back, he did the button I'd undone back up, and took his belt off. I watched as he undid his belt and pulled it out of the loops. I winced, remembering what leather felt like against my flesh, but before he could ask about my reaction, I reared up and shoved my hand into the opening he'd created, pushing my way past trousers and boxers.

"Fuck," he hissed, dropping his chin to the top of my head. "What the fuck?"

"No affection, remember?" I said, fisting him in a firm grip.

He was hot, searing. He was so hard, I could feel every ridge and vein in his cock and my mouth watered. It had been months, an entire year since…

Carter pushed me back to the mattress with his hand around my throat. He was gentle, unlike the last time he'd taken hold of my neck. His actions were no less powerful. He was unknowingly wiping thoughts of Michael from my mind, stopping me every time my thoughts edged towards my ex, and replacing them with himself.

"Foreplay is half the fun, babe," he said, reaching over to grab a condom from his bedside cabinet.

"Foreplay is overrated," I lied.

"Who are you?"

"Your match," I said, before taking the condom from him and tearing the packet with my teeth. "You've met it, *babe*."

Carter shook his head before a hiss left him when I tugged him free and rolled the condom down his impressive length.

"Don't unman me," he said, forcing me back into the mattress, his alpha aggression leaking through when he realised I'd taken control. "It'll end badly for both of us."

"Maybe that's what I'm bargaining on."

Was I? I had a death wish, I knew that; I had done since everything that made me who I was had been stolen from me. But did I want to die in the throes of passion, never to have another orgasm since Michael had-

"Forget him," Carter growled. I gasped when he fisted the base of his cock, and I wrapped my legs around him when he eased into me. "Don't think of another fucking man when I'm balls deep inside you."

"How did you-"

"Shh..." He silenced me with a kiss that was neither loving nor hateful. It just tore me up inside when I realised he was replacing Michael--again. "Just do as you're told, Harley."

Nodding, I closed my mouth and allowed myself to just feel. Carter was so thick, so hard and unforgiving as he stretched me and filled me and made me cry out in unrestrained pleasure. My nails clawed into his back, my feet dug into his ass, and I rocked against him as he picked up a rhythm that set my heart beating erratically. He sat back on his heels, gripping my hips to pull my body onto his as the angle stroked my g-spot and set my soul on fire.

"Are you thinking of anyone but me?" he grunted, glimmering sweat trickling from his temples.

"No."

"Are you thinking of anything besides my cock inside you until you forget your own name, let alone his?"

"No."

Why the sudden possessiveness? Why the sudden jealousy for something he'd only assumed, with no evidence to confirm his assumptions? Fuck, I didn't know, but I felt like he was screwing with me. Why? Why was he doing this? Why had he chosen me when he could have any pick of women who would bow to his whim?

"Harley," he growled, leaning over me to squeeze my breast through my clothing.

"What?" I bit, reaching to caress his pecs, digging into them until crescent shapes creased his shirt.

"Snap out of it."

"Then fuck me, Carter. Fuck me as if you hate me like I know you do." My hands slid around him to squeeze his ass. "Shut up and make me come."

Jesus, he was an animal, spurred on by me bruising his ego. He pounded into me again and again, until my head hit the headboard and my body built to a crescendo that would tear me apart.

"I'm coming!" I cried, throwing my head back into the pillow as my back arched. "God, Carter."

"That's it, babe," he whispered on a grunt as his thumb found my clit. "Come for me."

I screamed as I detonated, my entire body trying to fuse to his and push him away as my orgasm seized me. He held me still as I trembled with aftershocks, until he found his own release, threw his head back, and I felt every jerk of his cock as he came with a loud growl.

Carter fell asleep. Not long after he'd torn the condom off and tossed it into the bin without even needing to look at where it was, he laid next to me and passed out. I ached. My core felt bruised with the aggression of my first fuck in over a year, but it was the ache in my soul that had me climbing out of bed before he could escort me out. I let myself out of his apartment, calculated exactly how much time I'd need to be able to summon the lift and get in before it descended without me, and I stepped out into the silent street. Taking my phone out of my bag, I texted Evan and Ben and told them I was alive, thoroughly fucked (with a winky face so they wouldn't jump into aftercare-mode), and that I was going home.

And then I hailed a taxi.

When I woke in the morning, it was to a faint tapping on the door. I got out of bed and pulled my dressing gown on, headed downstairs one blurry step at a time, and opened the door expecting to see Evan with a coffee.

There was coffee held out in front of me, but not in the hands of either of my best friends. Instead, the should have been one-night-stand Carter held out a Starbucks cup. Inhaling the scent told me he'd brought me a caramel macchiato—my favourite.

"Heavy night?" he asked with a smirk.

I closed the door slightly to look in the mirror behind it. I looked like shit. I'd crawled into bed last night—early this morning—without taking my makeup off, and it was streaked down my face. My hair was up in a knot but sweat-matted clumps were evident.

"What do you want?" I asked, taking the coffee and closing the door around me so he couldn't burst in. "I thought we agreed one night."

"We did?"

"I didn't agree to your terms. I told you one night. I didn't buy into your 'let's see who wins' bullshit."

"My what?" He frowned, then it turned upside down into a shit-eating grin. "Ohh, I see. I'll win, Harley. I always do."

"Whatever. What do you want? I'm game to pretend it never happened if you'd prefer. In fact, I've forgotten it already, but I don't know why you're here."

"I thought we'd go for a run."

I snorted a laugh. "You don't know much about hangovers, huh?"

"So you were drunk last night?"

"Anyone would assume I'd been underneath someone else last night."

He chuckled and ran his hand through his hair. "Yeah. Well, drunk chicks aren't usually my thing. I made an exception for you." He winked. "So. Run. You've got coffee, I'm ready to go. Go and put that tight little arse in some running gear and we'll go."

I didn't want to go. Yes, I did. Carter in training gear was almost as hot as watching his face contort as he pumped into me. I pouted, knowing I would give in, but wondering if I'd made a mistake in going to bed with him last night. My mind was reeling, calling for something more than a run, but I wasn't sure Carter would take kindly to me calling my dealer and getting high in front of him. He hadn't earned my trust and I didn't need a lecture. I knew what I was doing.

"I'll be five minutes," I said, stepping back and closing the door.

"Can't I come in?" he called through it.

I didn't answer him. No, he couldn't come in. He was in far enough and I had to find a way to get him out of my system. I had to be patient and wait for him to fade, just like Cloud did whenever we had a session.

It was only a matter of time.

Eleven
HARLEY

The run helped to clear my head. I wouldn't let Carter know that though. I admitted—to myself—that I ran behind him to watch his tight arse move perfectly in the silky material of his shorts, although I called out at some point that I didn't want him to think a woman could outrun him. God forbid I bruised his ego more than I had last night.

The arousal at being so close to him again poured adrenaline into my muscles as sweat beaded on my brow. My calves tightened, my lungs ached, and just as I hit my stride, Carter veered off to the side into an alleyway.

I frowned, but followed, not wanting to break off now that my body had accepted it was time to exercise. Tall grass and nettles battered my legs but I kept up with him, my eyes scanning the isolated area for danger. My ears pricked at the only sound, our heavy footfalls on the gravelly path.

Carter stopped abruptly and my feet skidded on the small stones as I tried to stop myself from running into the back of him. Bending and holding my knees, I panted, trying to catch my breath.

"Why have we stopped?" I asked, looking up at him.

He didn't appear to be out of breath and I was more than impressed with his stamina. He reached into his pocket and pulled out a small square of foil.

My mouth fell open and I narrowed my eyes on the condom he flicked between his fingers. "Presumptuous, Carter."

He grinned, stepping into me and guiding me back against the wall. "I'm calling it the Harley effect, babe."

My chest was still heaving as I pulled much needed air into my lungs. One of his large hands circled my throat, making an inhale near-impossible.

"Sweat and sex," he murmured as he drew his nose up the side of my neck, the tip of his tongue following the trail and causing goose bumps to break out over my hot skin. "My favourite combination. Especially on your sweet, tight body."

"Carter." It was supposed to be a warning but his name came out breathy and, mortifyingly, with a small needy moan.

Taking that as some sort of validation, Carter grabbed the tops of my arms and spun me around, slamming the front of my body against the harsh brickwork. His hard cock dug into the base of my spine as his teeth grazed up the side of my neck. "Hard. Fast. Blunt and brutal," he declared as he yanked down my shorts.

I wanted to stop him. I wanted to fight him and tell him no. Yet, I couldn't. Not one part of me didn't want this as much as Carter.

The sound of the quick rip of foil filled the narrow space and he was balls deep inside me within seconds, my pussy stretched to its limit the further he pushed inside me.

We both growled and my teeth sank into my lower lip at the sound of my own animalistic groan.

"Shit," he hissed.

His forehead dropped to my shoulder and he started to fuck me with a raw power that left my legs shaking, my bones melting, and my lungs grappling for oxygen.

"Hot and so… Fucking… Tight," Carter murmured between thrusts as he snatched my hands and held them to the wall, the flat of my palms scraping over the rough stone.

Words left me as he pummelled me, his cock driving so deep and fast that every part of me felt the friction he created.

My breasts squashed against the wall the harder Carter pressed into me and I turned my face to the side to stop him from breaking my nose with the force of his thrusts. Bliss slipped into my body as each stroke in and out of me pushed me higher and higher.

"I need you to coat my cock in cum, Harley. Don't disappoint me."

Releasing one of my wrists, he slid his hand down and pinched my clit. My cry was loud and feral as ecstasy slammed into me, my body bucking wildly as my orgasm tore through me.

Carter snarled in my ear and forced himself so far inside me I swear I no longer existed as an individual. His pelvis pinned me to the wall as he came as hard as me, his breaths in my ear sharp and quick as he rode his climax.

I used the wall to hold me up as Carter used me, both of us fighting to level out our breathing and come back down to earth.

"You didn't beg," he finally whispered in my ear once his lungs had refuelled. "You know what that means."

I rolled my eyes, pushing him back so I could yank my shorts back up. "You want me to get on my knees and beg? Here? Now?"

He chuckled, "Now where's the fun in that?"

I tutted when he whipped off the condom and threw it into the tall grass that ran along the edge of the path. "I thought you were a neat-freak."

He looked perplexed for a moment but then shrugged my comment off. Grabbing my hand, he started to jog, pulling me behind him as my trembling legs struggled to keep up with him.

"Coffee."

"Home," I argued.

He looked over his shoulder, finally letting my hand go when I tugged at it. "Sure."

We ran in silence all the way back and when we finally ran up the path to my front door, Carter snatched the keys out of my hand and let me in.

He grinned when I pushed past him and glared.

"When I said home," I grumbled, "I meant alone."

"Such a drama queen." He sighed dramatically as he followed me into the kitchen, the deep frown on his face as he took in most of the broken furniture making my teeth clench. "What the fuck happened here?"

"You don't remember us tearing up my house last night?" I asked, quirking a brow and kicking off my shoes. "I know I said I wanted to forget, but this is getting ridiculous."

Carter paled and edged back towards the front door, his Adam's apple bobbing harshly when he forced himself to swallow.

"Gullible old shit."

Laughing, I turned and walked towards the counter.

"Funny." I gripped the edge of the worktop when Carter's mouth touched my neck, his hands on my shoulders. "I should punish you for playing such a cruel trick."

"It wasn't a trick. Anyone would think you get sexual amnesia."

"Oh no, babe. I remember your cunt very well, and I won't be forgetting it any time soon." I shook my head and rolled my neck as his lips fused to my flesh. "Now, are you going to tell me what really happened?"

"Nope." I shrugged him off, grateful when he stepped back and gave me the space I needed. "I have no reason to tell you."

"Was someone here? Or did you freak out and trash your own home?"

Did he really believe I'd done this? No, he didn't. He knew it was someone else, he knew my home had been invaded, and the son of a bitch had the audacity to try and make me look like a crazy to hide his own protective urges.

"I did it, of course."

"Tell me the truth, Harley Queen."

My body locked up and the kettle dropped from my grip onto the floor, the smash unheard through the buzzing in my ears. My brain physically burned as the name ricocheted off every lobe, taunting me, mocking me. My throat closed in and suddenly I couldn't breathe, my lungs wrestling with the shock coursing through me.

"Harley?" Carter's soft voice hardly penetrated, but his touch did as he gently led me over to the table and guided me onto a chair.

He dropped to a crouch in front of me, the worry in his gaze soft yet stern. "Breathe, babe. It's okay, you're safe."

My head shook and my body vibrated with terror. Finding my voice, I choked out, "Don't ever call me that again."

He nodded slowly. "Okay. My bad." He raised his hands to show he meant no harm. I scoffed. "I'm sorry."

"Why won't you leave me alone?"

He blinked at me and exhaled loudly. "I'm not quite sure I can give you an answer to that."

Running his thumb over my bottom lip, gently pulling it away from my teeth, he sighed. "What the fuck did he do to you?"

I halted and my breath stopped with my catatonic state. Why was he asking such a ridiculous question? Did he honestly expect me to answer it? Where had his suspicions come from, and why couldn't I lie to him and tell him he was wrong? A part of me wanted to let him in—the sane part of me screamed at me to run away.

"You need to go."

Anger lit his eyes with my brush off. But, surprisingly, he nodded. "Sure."

I couldn't figure out if I'd enraged him, or hurt him. Both emotions glared back at me for the few seconds that he remained staring at me. Then, without another word, he upped and left, pulling the door closed quietly behind him.

The itch in my blood, the memories invading my agonised mind, the tears that scorched my cheeks, could only be halted by one thing.

And it wasn't until the very next day that the coke-induced oblivion slipped away and once again the self-hatred crept back in.

Twelve
CARTER

If she wanted me to leave, I'd leave. I should have known she wouldn't be different, just because *I'd* been hired to kill her, and *I'd* decided to save her—at least for now. Why would that make *her* different to all the fucking others? Answer: it wouldn't.

I left her house without looking back, closing the door behind me and leaving her to whatever mind fuck she had going on in her head. I didn't want to be a part of it, just so I could get some ass and a tight pussy. No chick was worth that much hassle.

Except…maybe she was. I stopped halfway down her street and turned to look back at her house. The autumn sun was beginning to dip low in the sky and Harley's house caught the first orange glint of sunset. I scanned every window I could see, but not once did she step up to one to look for me. I knew something plagued her; I knew something tortured her memories and kept her locked somewhere in the past. The way Jack had mouthed *Mikey's girl* as if she were nothing more than just that—someone's property—had told me everything I needed to know about Harley Davids.

She didn't just need protecting from me.

Pulling my phone out of my pocket as I rounded my car and slid into the driver's seat, I scrolled through my contacts.

"Jace," I clipped when the head of security for Chimera answered my call.

"Carter? What's up, boss?"

"I need a little help. Off the record, and I'll double payment."

"Anything. What do you need?"

I'd found Jace at another club, when I'd been out doing some market research and sizing up my competitors before development on Chimera began. He'd been standing at the door, his brains and qualifications forgotten as he ticked names off a list on a clipboard and was left to decide if someone met the expectations of what the photographers inside wanted. I'd stopped to talk to him on my way out, having gathered all the information I needed, and he'd secured a job with twice the salary within three minutes of me stepping out of the doors.

"I need around the clock surveillance." Jace knew nothing about my *other* job, and I would keep it that way, thinking on the fly to keep him in the dark. "A friend of mine has been having some trouble with an ex. I want eyes on her every second of the day..." Backtracking, I let the unwelcome possessiveness commandeer my ability to speak. "Every *decent* second of the day. I want the names and files of everyone who comes into contact with her."

"Yes, boss. Do we make contact?"

"Absolutely not."

I gave him Harley's details and he agreed to have himself, or his assistant, Terry, on Harley's tail at all times, watching her six and keeping her safe while I worked to unlock her secrets. If she wasn't going to let me in, I was going to break in.

"What did you get up to last night?" I asked Jobe as I grabbed a bottle of beer and slumped on the sofa opposite him.

"Ah, you know." He tilted his head from side to side. I rolled my eyes. "Worked the bar for a while, met a pretty blonde and fucked her in the bathroom."

"Blonde?" I asked, taking a swig of beer. "They're not usually your thing."

"Neither is banging in a bathroom covered in piss and puke, but we work with what we've got, mate."

I laughed, shaking my head when he sparked up a joint.

"You have to do that in here?"

He shrugged. "Are you going to send me out into the rain like a dog?"

"Nope," I said, throwing my arms over the back of the sofa.

The best way to deal with Jobe was to *not* deal with Jobe. It was best to let him do his thing, search for his kick, and I knew he'd soon get bored when he realised I wasn't taking the bait.

"So," he said, hiding his shock when I leaned forward and plucked the joint from him. "How's...what's her name?"

"Harley."

"Yeah. How's Harley?"

Now, here was my dilemma. Harley had pissed me the fuck off...I'd checked my phone at least a hundred times throughout the day before I realised she didn't even have my number. What kind of girl screwed a man and didn't even attempt to stay in touch? None I'd ever been with. I wanted to toy with her. I wanted to lay her modesty out on the table between Jobe and me, and allow us to both laugh at the weak little woman who had fallen into the trap that was our life. The other part of me—the part I was least familiar with—wanted to keep what we had a secret. Secrets were the way to happiness. Keep the world out and no one could screw it up for you.

"Does it take you that long to scroll through the archives and remember a woman?" Jobe said with a laugh.

Instead of answering him right away, I sat back and took a draw, remembering just how competent weed was at clearing a raging mind. Two puffs and I felt like I was floating, and I laid my head back on the sofa.

"She's hot. She fucks like a whore and she kicks me out like a dude."

"Sounds too good be true."

"She is. If anyone knows that, it's us."

Jobe clinked his beer against mine and snatched his joint back. "I thought you didn't like the stuff."

"I don't."

"But..."

"Sometimes we have to do things we don't like."

"An example if you please, oh cryptic one."

"Like killing someone we want to protect. Or protecting someone we want to kill."

"Making a tough choice is half the fun."

Jobe sat forward, the evil glint in his eyes reflecting back at me as he rested his elbows on his knees and offered me his joint. I stared at it for what felt like forever. I stared at it like it was the choice I had to make, like somehow it would give me the answer and grant me possession of my balls once again. It didn't. Instead the wisps of smoke reminded me of the sway of Harley's hips and...I missed her.

Fucking women. They were only good for one thing.

"It sure is," I finally said, reaching out to take another hit.

Harley Davids didn't see many people in twenty-four hours. She hadn't moved from the kitchen the day she'd sent me away. Jace had arrived almost immediately and determined she'd been sleeping on the kitchen floor. She'd finally stood up once darkness had fallen and stumbled to bed, climbing beneath the bed sheets fully-clothed. It pissed me off that she'd slept on the floor, tucked up in the corner against the cupboards, surrounded by her broken furniture in her invaded home. Burglaries didn't have to result in chaos; I knew better than anyone that it was more than possible to break into a house and leave no trace. It pissed me off because I wanted to protect her. Not only could I not do that because I was actually supposed to *take* her life, but because she wouldn't let me. She'd opened me up to something I hadn't experienced for a long time and then she pushed me away to make me feel ashamed for having *hope*.

"We have a fella called Evan Gordon. He and the subject-"

"Harley."

"Yes." Jace cleared his throat. "He and Harley appear to be close. I'm forwarding you his image and profile, along with those of a Ben Sharpe. He, too, seems to be friendly with Harley. Neither of them appear to pose a threat, and she hasn't left the house yet."

"Stay on her."

"Of course."

I ended the call and continued to tap away at my keyboard. Harley had found her Number One somewhere, and I knew we had three more to go. *We.* I should have stepped away—far, far away—but I couldn't. Instead, I was finding out everything I could about Jack Forbes, and all his known associates. He'd been a snake. I sniggered when I thought about the irony—I was sure he was buried somewhere now, being eaten by the bacteria who would be eaten by the bugs who fed the worms that snakes fed on. It almost made me laugh out loud, but then I stumbled upon his criminal record. One Jack Forbes had been to prison ten times in his forty-two years of wasted existence. Turns out he was a dirty fucking rapist drug dealer, and *Ariel15* had done the world a favour when she ordered his hit. I broke into a few more databases, hacked into a few more archives and compiled a list of everyone Jack would have met in prison, people he was arrested with, who he'd stayed with during his many phases of probation, and anyone else who was mentioned in any of the files on any of the platforms I spent the entire day searching. One name popped up and burned itself into my memory. I suddenly had something to focus on. This hit had become more than personal. It had become everything.

I wouldn't search him yet. I wouldn't dive into his life unannounced and take every detail about his existence as if I owned it. I still had to find and extinguish Numbers Two and Three. Then, and only then, would I allow myself to find him and make him wish he'd never set eyes on Harley Davids.

Michael McKenzie.

"Dude, you need to sleep."

Jobe let himself into the office and when I looked up from the screen, I swear I saw my exhaustion bouncing back from him. We'd always been in sync; when he was stressed I got the headache. When I was running on fumes he could barely lift a cigarette to his lips. I guess we'd gotten lucky like that, but tonight he wouldn't agree. His dark eyes were hooded with tiredness as he glared at me.

"I will. I'm almost done."

"It's-" he looked at the time on his phone. "3am. Last time I came to check on you, at one, you were just finishing up. You've been almost done since eight this morning. Time to stop."

"I can't."

"What the fuck is the issue anyway?" he asked, sitting down on the seat next to me—the one reserved for when we needed to pull together. "Harley? Dude, you can't be serious."

"I'm deadly serious. I need to figure this out."

"No. We know how this is going to go. You're going to do your job, and we'll both have a little fun in the interim."

"What if I can't?"

"Can you?"

I thought about it, and scrubbed at my eyes. Maybe he was right. Maybe I was tired, confused, definitely not thinking straight, and I needed to get over it.

"Yeah." I laughed, shutting down my computer. "Of course I can."

"Good." He smacked my back as he stood up and waited for me to follow. "Now, go and knock one out so we can both get some sleep. Forget about this girl...she's just got you riled up because she's your first."

"You're right," I said, raising my hand to show him where my fist and I were going to avoid this conversation. "She's just another chick."

"Yep!" He laughed, throwing his hands up in triumph. "And I can't wait to fuck her into next week."

Thirteen
HARLEY

Vanessa smiled up at me as I leaned over the gallery reception desk. "The holidays you asked for are fine."

She grinned and clapped with excitement. "Yay. John's been looking at this little lodge in Snowdonia."

"Snowdonia? At this time of year?"

"Exactly this time of year."

Shrugging, I frowned when she looked over my shoulder and groaned quietly.

"Harley."

I curled a lip before planting a smile on my face and spinning around to face Bill Clancy. The man was persistent, I'd give him that. "Mr Clancy, what a pleasure."

His eyes roved down me, the image of sex in his eyes as he practically raped me with a single gaze over my body. Finally, eventually finding my face, he smiled. "I heard on the grapevine that you have a new Strovosky piece in."

"Then you heard correct." I swung an arm towards the front of the gallery, gesturing for him to follow me. "I must say," I spoke loudly, deliberately keeping my eyes away from him. "It's one of his finest. I think this particular watercolour will be highly sought after."

I could feel him staring at my backside and I cringed inwardly as his leer burnt through the material of my skirt.

Coming to stand before the exhibited canvas, I stiffened when Bill stood far too close to me, his arm brushing my hip and sending a quiver of revulsion into my sour stomach. Stepping aside, I swallowed back the bile. "The landscape is very personal to Strovosky, the image taken from the terrain…" I took another step back when Bill took another closer. My skin began to crawl with invisible insects, nausea making me blow out a steadying breath the closer he got to me. "…that surrounds his own private villa in…"

"Harley." Bill's voice was low and phlegmy, the sound making me want to gag. "When are you going to give in?"

I shuddered, unable to hide the reaction from his close proximity. "Mr Clancy, I…"

"I know you want me." He lifted a hand and ran the backs of his fingers down my arm. "We could have so much fun together."

Quickly, snatching my arm away from him, I stumbled slightly and grabbed onto the rope barrier that stretched across the front of the canvas.

A hand came from nowhere, fingers curling around the top of my arm and pulling me gently into a body. "Darling, there you are." Carter leaned down and pressed his lips to mine. "Open," he demanded quietly.

I did as he asked, instantly parting my lips for his tongue to slide against mine. He moaned on a breath, the faint flurry of warmth tingling on my tongue.

Finally breaking away, his kiss leaving me breathless and needing to hold onto the barrier even harder, he blinked at Bill as though he hadn't seen him stood beside us. "Ahh, Bill. How are you?"

He slipped an arm around my waist and pulled me possessively into his side, his fingers digging into my hip almost painfully.

"I didn't know you two were an item," Bill spat, his glare on Carter's dominant caress.

"Oh, did you not?" He looked down at me, his eyes twinkling and a soft smile curving his mouth. "Yes. How long is it now, Harley, darling?"

"Uhh, around six or seven weeks." I smiled up at him, trying my best to mirror his affectionate gaze.

"In fact, if you'll excuse us, Bill, I've come to steal my gorgeous woman away for lunch."

Without allowing Bill a retort, he grabbed my hand and directed me over to the staff door that led to the gallery office.

"Code," he growled when I stood mute and stunned.

Nodding and pulling myself out of the haze, I punched in the door code, not caring that Carter watched every press of the keys. It was easy to change it.

"Well here we are again," he smirked as soon as we entered the office and he kicked the door closed behind me.

I shook my head, holding up a finger and retreating backwards. "Sex is out. I have a lunch date."

Rage, or distrust, I couldn't figure out which, flashed in each unique, but very stunning eye. "Oh?"

He stepped into me, pressing me into the wall. My neck ached as I looked up at him. "My life doesn't revolve around you, Carter. Yes. I have a date."

The fury that flowed from him made my throat constrict, and not knowing why, I swiftly amended my statement. "But not like you think."

His glare faded and he grinned. "Good girl. I'd think long and hard about even deliberating fucking another man."

My eyes widened. "Excuse me? Who the hell are you to tell me what I can and can't do?"

I gasped when he pinched my nipple through the silk of my blouse, a shot of pleasure spiralling through me and making me shiver beneath his sharp touch.

Fire heated his eyes, turning green and blue into need and lust. Placing his hands on my hips he slowly slid the material of my skirt upwards, bunching it over my hips. "I'm the one you're going to get down on your knees for."

His eyes dropped and a grin sneaked across his face when he took in my stocking tops. Cupping my pussy, he pressed his index finger against my clit and sent a shot of hunger through me.

"You're a bastard," I breathed, already squirming against his hand, needing him to placate the ache that was becoming unbearable.

"The bastard whose cock is going to slide between those pretty pink lips and choke you."

My teeth snapped together when his hands settled on my shoulders and he slowly pushed me to crouch before him.

Glaring at him, hating what he was able to do to me, I lifted a hand to his trousers and unhurriedly tugged at his zip. "You want me to gag on your cum, Carter?"

He hissed, moving his hands from my shoulders to my hair and snaking the length around his fist when I took out his cock and curled my fingers around him. His eyes bore down on me as I gazed up at him and very slowly sank my lips down the entire length of him.

"Jesus!" he growled. "Do you not have a gag reflex?"

I smirked, cupping the underside of him with my tongue and sucking hard. His teeth sank into his lip as he watched me blow him, his hands in my hair tightening with every slow but long pull on his cock.

Pre-cum tickled my taste buds and Carter suddenly yanked me upwards. Slamming my back against the wall, he lifted my legs around him while he tore into a condom with his teeth. I wanted to laugh as I watched him struggle to slide it over his cock while my legs were wrapped around his body, restricting his vision and his movements.

But all humour left me when he slammed into me right to the hilt. His balls pressed against me, his teeth found my neck, and his growl in my ear made my head fall back and my pussy grip him like a vice.

"Always so fucking tight, Harley," he uttered as he slowly slid out of me and then plunged back in, the sheer force of his drive slapping my body harshly against the wall.

"That all you got?" I taunted, winking at him when fire blazed his eyes.

"I'm not sure you can handle what I've got, babe."

I laughed, riling him further. "Try me."

Gasping when his hand circled my throat tightly, abruptly cutting off my air, he forced himself so far inside me I saw stars.

"Fuck!" I groaned.

My eyes closed and Carter started to fuck me with a raw power I was struggling to ride through. His thrusts were hard and painful but so fucking good. His talk was filthy and degrading but such a turn on. His hunger was as potent as mine and I fell into the cocoon of pleasure he was forcing on me. The world around me stopped, the air in my lungs froze and every thought in my head left me when only ecstasy commandeered every part of me. Pleasure seeped into my bones, driving me higher and higher as my muscles strengthened in preparation for the orgasm Carter was demanding of me.

It wasn't until I heard Carter's sharp gasp that I realised he'd stopped.

It was then I felt the rush of cold air across my chest.

My eyes snapped open and I froze when I realised Carter had ripped open my blouse.

"What the...?" His voice was quiet but tight, his shock restricting his airway and making him high-pitched.

"No!"

I slapped at him, trying to force him away from me.

Pure fury leaked from him as his distressed gaze slowly moved from my chest to my eyes. "Who the fuck did this?"

"No!" I slapped at him again, squeezing my eyes closed as I tried to clamp down the tears that were burning my retinas. "No!"

I fought against him when he gripped the centre of my bra and ripped it open, baring my naked, and very scarred, breasts to his furious stare.

His eyes snapped up to mine and I whimpered at the feral growl that tore from him. "Who – the – fuck – did – this – to – you?"

Finding a strength I didn't know I had, I pushed him. He stumbled back and allowed me a little leeway to stand and dip under his arm. "Get out!"

"Harley." He was distraught, his hand reaching for me but I yanked my blouse back around me, covering myself, and shook my head.

"GET OUT!"

Uncertainty made him step towards me again but I shook my head.

"Please." My tears choked me. "There. I'm finally begging." My throat ached, but not as much as my heart. "I'm begging you, Carter. You got what you wanted. Please. Go."

Without another word, he zipped himself up and left.

He'd wanted me to beg. I'd wanted him to leave me alone. Yet, now both had come at once, I wasn't sure I wanted the outcome.

Fourteen
CARTER

Jobe peered over my shoulder as my fingers flew across the keyboard, every now and then moving to pick up the pen and jot down another name.

"What's going on?" he asked, picking up the notepad and scanning the list of names.

"I need to find out who this fucker is."

"Which fucker?" He chuckled. "We know a lot of fuckers."

I glanced at him before turning back to concentrate on the task at hand. "You have any clue who hired us to terminate Harley Davids?"

Jobe sighed. "Shit. Dude, what the fuck is it with this chick? She's just a cunt. Ride it, end it."

His eyes snapped wide when I spun around and lunged for him. "The bastards fucking carved 'whore' across her fucking tits. The cunts buried into her fucking flesh with fucking smokes. The motherfuckers ripped her to fucking bits!"

His mouth moved but no words left him. Shaking his head slowly, he took my hands from around his throat and gently lowered them. His eyes glinted as his chest heaved against mine. "Then get back to work," he growled, snatching his phone from his back pocket. His eyes fixed hard on mine as he spoke into it. "Jimmy, need a favour, mate."

I turned back to the screen, scrolling down the list of inmates at Belmarsh prison.

My own phoned buzzed and I snatched it up when Jace's name scrolled across the screen. "Yep."

"You're not gonna believe this," he said.

"Fill me in."

"She's just met with Jimmy Sheldon."

My eyes snapped to Jobe and I made a cutting motion across my throat, signalling for him to end his call.

So Jimmy Sheldon had been Harley's lunch date. I shouldn't have been as happy about that as I was. I knew their relationship was purely platonic; Jimmy no longer owned a cock since his last stretch inside had seen it hacked off by some crazy motherfucker.

"What?" Jobe asked when he did as I asked and terminated the connection.

"When, where?" I snapped at Jace.

"They're both currently sat in the far corner of the local fucking Costa."

"Are you kidding me?"

"Nope." He laughed quietly. "He sat down, she got up to get drinks and then he moved across to her seat. He took the carrier bag she'd left under the table and shoved it in his backpack, then he dropped a similar one to the floor in its place."

"Keep on her." My eyes narrowed on nothing as I shut my phone off. "She's using Jimmy." I said mindlessly to Jobe.

125

He frowned and reared back. "What the fuck does she want with Jimmy?"

My eyes slowly moved to the list of names I had constructed and quickly roamed over them. The name next to the very last one smacked me in the face. "I can't believe I missed it."

"Missed what?"

"Fucking Jimmy's dad. He's in Belmarsh."

"And?" he queried, taking the chair next to me.

"Along with Number Two on Harley's list."

"I didn't know she'd you sent a number two."

I laughed, grinning. "Not yet she hasn't."

As if my girl -*my girl?* – was in the very room with me, my IM pinged instantly.

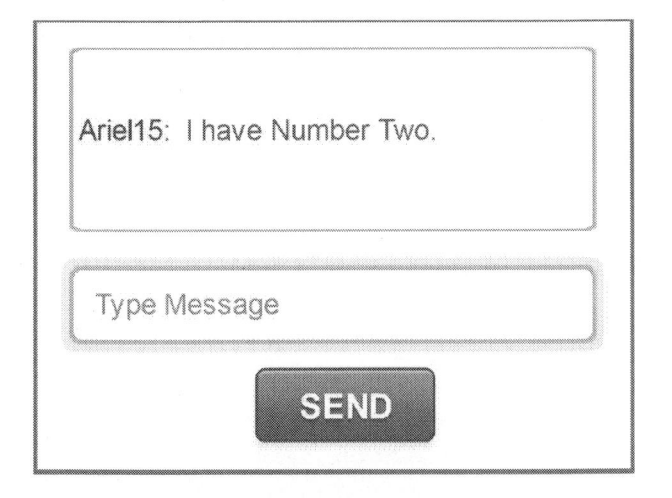

Ariel15: I have Number Two.

Type Message

SEND

"Clever girl." I grinned with pride when an email deposited itself in my secure inbox. She'd used Jimmy to give me an opening, notifying me that because Number Two was in Belmarsh it was still possible for me to get to him.

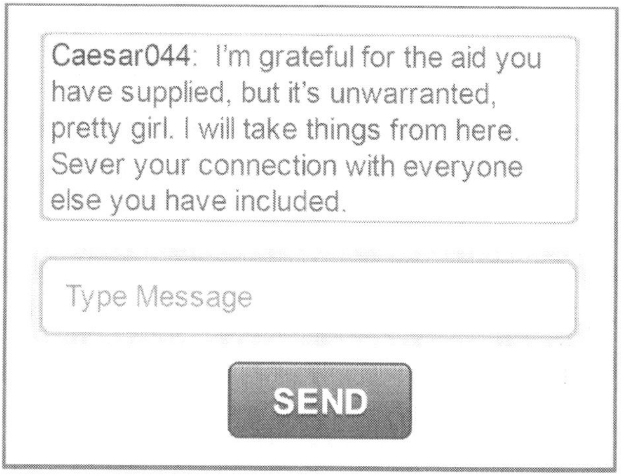
Caesar044: I'm grateful for the aid you have supplied, but it's unwarranted, pretty girl. I will take things from here. Sever your connection with everyone else you have included.
Type Message
SEND

There was a pause, before she conceded.

Ariel15: I'm sorry, I was just trying to help. Done.
Type Message
SEND

Her quick surrender told me she still wasn't herself after what had happened that morning. Visions of her mutilated breasts burned more rage through me and I bit my lip with guilt for being so stern with her.

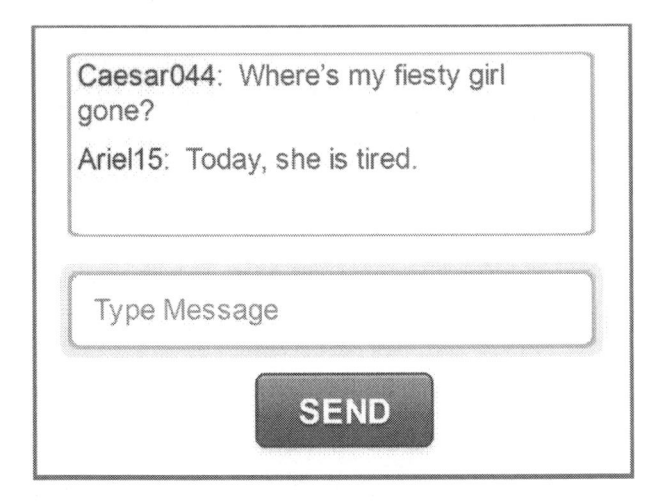

> **Caesar044**: Where's my fiesty girl gone?
>
> **Ariel15**: Today, she is tired.

Type Message

SEND

My throat hurt when the connection ended and my chat box shut down. I had hurt her with my reaction. Except, I wasn't exactly sure how she wanted me to react, or what I was supposed to have done and said. The fuckers had torn her to bits, shredded her soft silky skin. Fury bubbled in my gut. I wanted to gut every one of them, rip out their insides and force each fucking rotten piece of flesh down their rancid throats.

My thoughts moved to the little box I kept securely hidden away, ready for when Harley Davids conceded to me, to who I was and what she had asked of me.

"Number Two gonna prove difficult?" Jobe asked sceptically.

I laughed, and shook my head. "Number Two is surprisingly easy."

He quirked an eyebrow. "Oh?"

"It's Charlotte's brother."

Air left his lungs in a sudden rush as he dropped to the couch, the mention of *her* name after so long stilling the beat of his heart. Pretty much like my own really.

Fifteen
HARLEY

I stared up at the ceiling as what felt like countless numbers of hands roamed my body. Except they weren't uncountable. Three pairs. Six hands. Twenty-four fingers and six thumbs. Every single one of them touched a part of me without my permission, but I no longer cared. I knew it had only been hours, but it felt like days. Days since my last hit. Days since I was last in possession of my own body. Days since I'd been lying in bed as the high wore off, waiting for Michael to return with the promise of another. Days since I'd felt like me. Right now I felt hollow, staring at the ceiling as I lost myself a little more. My legs were held around a large body as a cock pummelled in and out of me. My hands were pinned down by knees as four fingers shoved their way into my throat to make me puke. The fingertips of another hand rubbed my clit furiously as if I was supposed to get some pleasure out of this. I laughed, rolling my eyes when I realised how far gone I was.

"Something funny, princess?" the leader asked, leaning over me to squeeze my breasts together.

I shook my head, refusing to talk. I knew they'd want a fight, and I'd give it to them—secretly. I'd sneak up on them and punish them all when this was over. If this was ever over.

"I don't think she understands the seriousness of her predicament," Number Two sneered as he flicked my nipples protruding between Number One's fat fingers.

"Do you know how many times you've gotten high because of us?" Number One asked. "Do you know how many IOUs we've taken from Mikey with the promise that payment is coming?"

I shook my head again, wincing when the third guy smacked my face. He laughed, slipping into his boss's place when another surge of cum filled me, signalling it was time for a changeover.

"Fifteen," he continued, sliding between the wet lips of my pussy. Somewhere in the back of my mind, I wondered if I was filled with the seed of as many orgasms from these pricks. "That means you've got fifteen instances to pay for."

"No," I choked past the fingers in my mouth, making me gag. "Please, no."

I promised I wouldn't beg, but I knew I would. I was weak. Michael had rewritten my genetic code, making me a nobody, after everything Daddy had done to make me a warrior.

"Ah, it's no good begging now, sweet thing," one of them mumbled—I wasn't even sure who was talking anymore. "It's decided. You're paying the debt and then we'll be out of your hair...if you survive."

"Please don't kill me," I whimpered as I watched the man thrusting away inside me light a cigarette. "Please."

I coughed as the smoke choked me, the fingers in my mouth finally granting me some mercy. My coughing brought the ache between my legs and deep inside my core to the forefront of my mind and, finally, I cried. I cried so hard, watching Michael standing in the corner knowing he was safe because I was paying for the both of us. I knew what the three men were hoping for—that they were punishing Michael by fucking me. The only problem was, he didn't care. He just stood there and watched and I swear I saw a hint of amusement in his dull, drug-ravaged eyes.

"Ready to count with us, Harley?" one of them asked as the other one took the cigarette from his mouth, blowing out a suffocating cloud of smoke as he rolled the white stick in his fingers.

"Count what?" I had the stupidity to ask.

I didn't ask again, not after the cherry of the cigarette made contact with my skin. I screamed when my flesh sizzled and the first scar branded my skin where it would stay forever.

I woke up in a cold sweat, my arms crossed over to dig my nails into my biceps. Dry heaves wracked my body when I remembered the pain of the fifteen cigarette burns I'd taken on my chest. I could still feel the intense sting, still smell my skin burning.

I shivered when the cold breeze from my open window whispered over the tiny crevices in my body, making me aware of the gaping craters in my soul. I physically shook with rage, not only at the four men who were responsible for breaking me and turning me into this...*thing*. But I felt rage for Carter too. I was so damn angry with him for breaking through my defences and then pushing me one step further when I'd made it clear the top half of my body remained covered. He hadn't answered my silent prayer, he hadn't taken my cues, and he hadn't respected my wishes. He'd torn them open when he ripped my blouse, and I didn't know how to find a way back to the numbness I needed to live in to survive. Throwing the covers off and pressing my head back into the pillow, I took a deep breath. I wanted him out of my life, and yet with him in it, I'd never felt so alive. He'd wanted me to beg, and that's exactly what I'd done. What was left now? An emptiness I didn't recognise as my safe place, and a loneliness I didn't want.

"Fuck this," I huffed, getting out of bed and hastily pulling on some clothes.

It was dark, I was cold; the lingering grogginess of sleep and the cocaine I'd snorted just a few hours ago made me hazy, and I didn't think before I left my room, then the safe confines of my home, and hailed a taxi.

"Carter doesn't take unexpected calls, doesn't welcome uninvited visitors, and doesn't appreciate being woken at such an ungodly hour," the man at the door said when I'd arrived and asked to go up to the penthouse.

"Please, he'll let me in."

"Then he should be here to take you up himself."

"Please."

Pursing his lips, the guy folded his arms and looked away as if I wasn't even there. "No can do."

"Fine."

I had two choices now. I either gave up and wasted more money on a taxi home, or I persisted and waited for Carter. I didn't know why I'd suddenly gone crazy stalker chick on him, but I couldn't help it. I wasn't myself; I hadn't been since he'd exposed my secrets earlier this afternoon and nothing I'd tried—nothing short of an overdose—would calm my chaotic mind. Deciding to take a breather and get my act together, I flipped off the doorman, dressed in ridiculous all black uniform, and turned away from Chimera. I didn't go far, only as far as the alleyway at the end of the street, before I let my failure consume me, and slumped to the ground against the wall. What kind of life was this? Not one I wanted. I was a successful business woman, making a name for myself on my own, as well as upholding a reputation I'd built myself in the virtual world, and yet, nothing I seemed to do, nothing I accomplished was enough. Not even the knowledge that I was a quarter of the way through my mission, with the images of Jack dead and almost skinless whirling around my mind. What else was there? What else could I do to fix this festering hole in my soul that just kept widening and widening with every day I made it through?

I reached into my bag and pulled out a pouch I'd saved for later. I always had a backup and I'd never been more grateful for it than tonight. With shaky hands, I poured the powder onto the back of my closed fist and hunched over to snort it. The second it travelled up my nostril and began streaming into my blood, I felt better. I felt a little bit more human. I felt like maybe this was where I was supposed to be, and what I was supposed to be doing—a junkie getting high, alone, in a dirty alleyway while people lived life to the full just metres from me.

"Harley."

I heard his voice through the haze and reached for him, but it was unnecessary. He was already crouching in front of me and slinking his hands into my hair to hold my head upright.

"I tried to get in," I slurred. "I just wanted to see you."

"I know, babe. I know." He cleared his throat. "I'm here now."

"They're just scars. They mean nothing."

"I don't care about the scars."

He chuckled and I remembered to be wary of him. There was something about Carter that told me to be careful. I didn't know why, I was never good at listening to my instincts and, once again, I chose to ignore them. When Carter offered me his hand, I took it and allowed him to help me stand.

"Let's get you upstairs."

There was a hunger in his voice no amount of intoxication could miss. I knew he wasn't going to take me upstairs, let me cry into one of his crisp white shirts, and cuddle me to sleep telling me everything was going to be okay. That wasn't the kind of man he was, and it wasn't the kind of relationship—or whatever it was—we had. I knew he'd take me up to his apartment, fuck me until I couldn't breathe without rippling around him in bliss, and then I'd get a taxi home in the morning and avoid him until the next time he magically appeared in my life. I refused to think of the comedown, and what would happen if I was still around him when I sobered up.

I giggled when we stepped out of the lift, Carter almost dragging me through the foyer and into his apartment. There was no time for talk tonight, there was nothing he wanted to say, and my stomach flipped with both fear and longing when I contemplated taking a punishing hate-fuck from him.

"Slow down," I whispered, shoving my hands to his shoulders to try and push him off me when he threw me to the sofa and tumbled down with me. "Carter, please."

"Hush now, babe." He pressed his finger to my lips. "There's no reason to talk."

"But—Oh!"

Carter ground against me, the hardness of his cock, the thickness and heat evident through his pyjama bottoms caught a spark between my legs and ignited into raging arousal. Rough hands grabbed my breasts, his teeth dug into my neck, heating the flesh with guttural groans and sharp breaths, and he pried my legs open with his knees to expose more of me to him.

"Such a bad girl," he hummed against my skin. "No knickers under the skirt, huh?"

I shook my head, feeling the need to explain myself, but I couldn't. I couldn't speak, and didn't want to. I just wanted to feel.

"Now," he said, leaning back with his hands on my stomach, nails digging into muscle to make me tense beneath him. "I think we should play a little game."

"I don't want to play a game. I just want to fuck."

"Nuh uh." Leaning down he placed a quick kiss to my lips before sitting back up. "It's for your benefit, babe."

"How?"

"Sometimes our senses trick us into thinking and feeling things we don't want to think or feel." He smirked, glancing down at my body. "I promise not to look at you while I make you come over and over again, but I want you to allow me to take the same steps."

"What?"

I shook my head. I had no idea what was going on. All I knew was I didn't care what he did to me; I just needed him to soothe this ache, extinguish this smouldering flame that made me need him more than my next breath.

"Let me show you."

He whipped off his vest, exposing a tight stomach decorated with toned abs and soft muscle, and a waist that narrowed to hips with a perfect V signalling where I wanted to go, calling to me like a beacon. His pecs were firm, but not unrelenting, his chest smooth, his collarbone making my tongue flex with the urge to slide over the dips and taste the saltiness of his skin.

"Carter…"

Looking at him, being beneath a body so perfectly in proportion and looked after, made me feel inadequate, and my eyes searched the area around me for my bag. Maybe I could persuade him to let me use the bathroom so I could rid myself of this self-loathing. Instead of granting me time, Carter gave me blindness, settling his vest over my eyes like a blindfold and securing it around the back of my head. I couldn't see a thing, but I could smell him. There was something about the virile scent of a man who worked hard and played harder that made my clit throb for attention, which Carter teased with another roll of his hips.

"Ready to play, Harley Davids?"

Without hesitation, I nodded.

Sixteen
CARTER

Charlotte. Once upon a time it had been a name I'd adored. One I'd whispered with love and roared with passion. One I'd called in my sleep, uttered when I woke, and groaned as I'd fallen asleep with images of her leading to a sticky hand.

Now it was a name I loathed. It was a name that instantly made me want to crush a windpipe and rip out the tongue of the person who said it. It was the name of the woman who had made me everything I was today—almost—and a name I would carry to my grave with hatred and resentment.

"Baby," Charlotte cooed as we passed the jewellery shop hand-in-hand. "Baby, please."

The way she said please made my dick hard, and my balls swelled in preparation for some fun. Some more fun after the two sessions of it we'd had in bed this morning. I had more sex than most nineteen-year-olds, and it was all thanks to my nymph of a girlfriend. I'd scored the gorgeous travel agent who sold me and Rome a holiday to Ibiza with a free upgrade, and while at the time I thought I'd take her out for a drink, sink my cock into her and get us both off a few times, I'd fallen in love with the chick. Like, sick, puppy love that made me ready to lay my life down for her, and hand her my balls on a platter if she asked.

But the necklace she pointed to as she stabbed her finger to the glass and glanced up at me with wide blue eyes was way out of my price range.

"How about this?" I started, wrapping my arm around her and pulling her snug against me. "We'll buy it as a celebratory piece. Once I've got Chimera up and running, bringing in the money like a pimp in Soho, I'll buy you the entire fucking shelf."

She sighed, but looked longingly into my eyes and, at the time, I thought it was in love and support.

"You're going to make it, baby," she said with a smile. "And then I want the whole fucking shop."

I'd bought the whole shop, of course I had, but I'd closed it down, and turned it into a sex shop before selling it to a Madame. I'd done it to spite her, to stop her buying any more shit—or using *him* to buy her any more shit. She'd well and truly pulled the wool over my eyes and it wouldn't happen again. This time I would use her to get my kicks, knowing she'd lead me straight to Number Two and I'd be able to punish the cunt and his slut of a sister the only way I knew how. With blood.

"Carter?" Alec, the doorman, called through the intercom and I crossed the room to answer it.

"What's up?"

"There's a chick down here for you. Says you'll let her in, but they all say that. She seems pretty messed up."

Rolling my eyes, I prayed it wasn't the girl from Friday night, back to try and convince me she didn't have a boyfriend who fucked her with less passion than a wet fish.

"She's gone," he continued. "But I'm worried about her safety. Something seems...off."

"I'm on my way down."

Three minutes later, I was stepping out into the street and looking down the length of it. Whoever had come with the hopes of a replay hadn't stuck around to play psycho.

"She seemed a little broken," Alec said, patting me on the shoulder. "Normal, though, which I guess is a new thing for you."

He laughed, but I remained still, looking through the crowd of people queuing to get in. I knew who Alec was talking about. I didn't know her, hardly at all, but I knew enough to know Harley had succumbed to whatever it was she felt, and had come to find me.

"I'll handle it," I said, stepping out when Alec pointed in the direction she'd taken.

It didn't take long to find her. She was crouched against the wall with her face to her knees and if my instincts hadn't told me she was pissed, I would have thought she'd fallen asleep.

"Harley."

She woke quickly, if resistant, and hazy vision searched for me in the dim light. I don't really know what happened next; I knew she was vulnerable and emotional, and that was my cue to take advantage. To find some way to punish her for what she'd done to me, and remind myself of the job I had to do. In no more than ten minutes, she was beneath me on the sofa, squirming as I pressed my cotton-covered cock against her bare pussy, with her face covered by my vest. I knew I wasn't alone tonight, and I knew it was time to up the ante.

"Ready to play, Harley Davids?" I asked, leaning back to pull my trousers down and grip my cock.

When she nodded without hesitation, I smiled. Play with her, I would. She cried out when I buried my face between her legs, and moaned when I swiped my tongue along the slit of her tight cunt, diving inside her to give us both a taste of what was to come. Her legs clamped around my head and I sucked on her clit with a pop when two hands pried them back open. I looked up and saw Rome standing over her, staring at me with a cocktail of rage and excitement in his eyes. One hand let go of her and he pressed his finger to his lips. I grinned, keeping my hands on my cock as I dived back into her pussy and he gripped her breasts in a rough hold that told me he wasn't sure we should be playing the game this close to home. To hell we shouldn't. This was the best way to do it…to get her the fuck out of my system. I didn't mind sharing my women. Charlotte had had no qualms taking on more than one man, so why couldn't every other woman who succumbed to my charm without ever searching for the real me, head in the same direction?

"Does that feel good, babe?" I asked, smirking when she twitched against me as I blew on her sensitive flesh.

"So good," she mumbled, reaching up to cover Rome's hands with her own.

He grinned. I grinned. Non-consensual threesomes were what I did best.

Rome nodded and I settled back, severing contact with Harley as Rome freed himself from his trousers.

"Ready to suck some cock, babe?"

"Yes." She arched her back, searching for me—or Rome—she had no fucking idea.

"Open wide."

She opened her mouth and, seizing hold of her throat, Rome yanked her back so her head hung over the arm of the sofa. He gripped the back of it and fisted his other hand on his hips as he slid into her mouth and I stood, shoving two fingers into her. She moaned and my cock reacted, calling for me to fist it and work it covertly as Harley sucked cock. She did it like a pro too; very little gag reflex and a shit-ton of dedication. She slurped and feasted, sucking up her own spit and taking Rome's cock all the way down her tight throat. I rubbed furiously at her clit, encouraging her to come for the both of us. The closer she got, the harder she sucked, and the wetter she'd be when I finally fucked her.

"So good, babe," I hissed, clearing my throat when the urge to laugh moved in. "You suck my dick so fucking good."

She whimpered an affirmative, some sort of thanks for a compliment on something I couldn't even feel, but the tensing of Rome's stomach and the bunching of his thighs told me he agreed. Rome pulled out of her mouth, blowing out a silent breath through puffed cheeks, and I covered her face with my hand when she attempted to remove the vest.

"Nuh uh," I chastised, smiling when Rome slapped her cheek. "We had a deal."

"Sorry," she murmured, squirming on the sofa, her beautiful ass pressing itself into the seating. "Please, Carter."

"Are you begging, Harley Davids?"

She froze, but finally a smirk decorated her blowjob-swollen lips. "You've made me beg once, why not do it again?"

"So, since you're begging, I should stop?"

"No!" She reached for me but Rome gripped her wrist.

"Then do as you're told and take it like a good girl."

She nodded, and I took the cue, moving onto the next stage. Rome stepped away as I resumed my position between her legs, wrapping them around me as I caught the foil packet making its way towards me. I winked at Rome, thanking him for having my back, and noticed him rolling another packet between his fingers like it was a lucky coin. When my cock was protected and Harley was damn near combusting with need, I let us both have it and drove into her in one fluid move.

"Ah," she sighed through parted lips, throwing her head back further off the sofa.

I almost wished she knew she was being violated, so I could watch her reaction when she took two cocks at once.

She was so hot, gripping me until I had to clench my teeth together to stop myself from spewing into her. I fisted my hands by my side, giving Rome the role of touch. He smirked at me, understanding the challenge I was under as I fought to stop myself coming so quickly. She lifted into me perfectly, taking my length like she was made for me, her cunt massaging every single fucking inch of me.

Rome slowly slid the material of her top upwards, revealing firm tits encased in regular white cotton. The sight of such simple underwear had my balls drawing in tight. Lace, silk, even fucking sheer gossamer shit had nothing on pure, angelic white cotton.

She fought with him, her hands slapping out but he placed his hand on her cheek and shushed her. "It's okay."

The sight of her scars made my gut clench, rage pouring into my veins and making me thrust hard inside her to compensate for the excess of adrenaline.

Her tits stood proud, and Rome, moving alongside me, lowered one cup of her bra. "You have beautiful tits, babe," he whispered, making her relax around me once again. But then taking a perky nipple in his mouth, he bit around it gently.

Harley groaned, lifting her hips and taking more of me inside her.

I smacked out at him but he chuckled silently, biting again and making the cum in my balls surge into the condom. Gritting my teeth to stop the growl that wanted to erupt, I dug my fingers into my thighs and rode the high, silently.

Rome took place behind me as I reached up and twisted Harley's nipples between my fingers, forcing her to concentrate on the pleasure as Rome took place between her sweet thighs.

She gasped, nearly choking on her own breath when he thrust deep and hard inside her, knocking her an inch up the couch.

He bit into his lip as we both stilled, praying she didn't notice the difference. But she was drowning in so much pleasure she wrapped her legs around him and took it.

I stood watching Rome bring her to orgasm again and again. There was a look in his eye as he fucked her with a fury that I hadn't seen from him in a long while. His gaze stayed on her chest, his eyes memorising every single fucking scar on her chest.

Fifteen burns.

Ariel **15**.

Fuck!

I kept my mouth shut. The adrenaline was sinking into sadness now that I'd fucked her into oblivion. They would all pay.

That, I would make damn sure of.

Blinking, I shook away my thoughts and watched as Harley's back bent and she came over

Rome's cock as he followed her over, a loud groan accompanying his climax.

His forehead dropped to her stomach and when I tapped him on the back, he stared up at me in confusion.

Pointing to the bedroom, realisation hit home, and he nodded, quickly pulling out of her. He gazed down at her for a moment, a deep frown creasing his brow but biting into his lip and sighing, he took one more look, then disappeared.

Waiting until he'd gone, I reached down and slipped my vest from Harley's eyes. Her mascara had run down her face, her cheeks were flushed, and her bottom lip was ravished from where she had bitten into it from so many orgasms.

She smiled. She fucking smiled, and I had to swallow the restriction in my throat.

"Better?" I asked softly, taking her hand and helping to pull her upright.

She nodded, a shyness creeping over her.

Laughing, I shook my head. "Why so shy all of a sudden?"

She shrugged, pulling her top down quickly and hiding her secrets once again. "Something was…." She mused over her words, then frowned to herself. "…Different."

"Different?"

She didn't clarify her statement, and instead, suddenly whipped up her clothes and started to pull them on. "I have to go."

"Really? Am I that bad?"

Her eyes widened and she shook her head quickly. "No… I…."

"I'm just winding you up. I have to get down to close the joint up anyway."

I'd never been with a woman who was ever in such a rush to leave after sex. It was a novelty, and one I wasn't sure I liked very much.

I watched her walk across the room and before she reached the hallway, she paused. "What…. What are we doing, Carter?" She didn't turn to look at me, just stood staring away from me.

She jumped when I came up behind her, brushing her long hair to the side to drop a kiss on the back of her neck. "Whatever we want. Don't overthink it, babe."

She nodded, her gulp loud. "Okay."

I frowned when the door clicked closed behind her. Rome stood in the bedroom doorway staring at me. "She knew."

I nodded. "Yeah. I think she did. But how, none of them ever have before?"

He sighed. "Experience." Walking back into the bedroom, he lowered his voice, except I still heard him. "And not from a good experience. So what exactly does that make us?"

Seventeen
HARLEY

Plum mewed at Evan when he pulled off the lid of her warm milk and placed it beside her on the worktop. Stroking his hand down her back, he narrowed his eyes on me. "Spill."

I shook my head and smiled, praying he let it go. But it was Evan, my best friend, the only person who could read me like a book. "I'm good."

"Then why do you look like you did way too much last night?"

I grimaced at the anger in his voice. Shrugging, I turned away, taking a sip of the coffee he'd brought, and took a seat at my workstation.

It had been three days since I'd stumbled into my house after the marathon sex session with Carter. With Carter—and his friend.

How could he think I wouldn't notice? I wasn't sure who I was angrier with, him or myself. The thing was, and the thing I couldn't get a grip on, I trusted him. He was dangerous, lethal even, yet something inside confirmed he would never hurt me, at least physically. I had a feeling he knew what had happened in my past. I didn't know if he did what he did because he wanted to exorcise those demons for me, or if he really thought I wouldn't figure it out and he'd totally violated me. I should have been outraged, sickened that I couldn't figure it out. Disgusted by what had happened, and the knowledge that a stranger had been inside me... yet I wasn't.

I squeezed my thighs together when feelings that refused to go away rolled over me once more, the memory of two different cocks inside me warming my belly with a heat I hadn't felt in a long time. In a way, Carter, unknowingly, had helped me to take the past and overwrite it with new sensations, a new mindset on having more than one man at the same time.

Evan understood my silence, but sighed heavily. "Did you manage to shift the records for the client?" he asked, changing the subject to one he knew I would accept.

"Yeah, simple hack. Cleared in sixteen minutes." I sighed. "Sometimes I wish we'd get a job that required some grit, instead of all this boring shit."

He laughed, and nodded in agreement. "Yeah, but hey, boring pays the bills."

My IM popped up in the right hand corner of my screen, and I frowned when the unfamiliar tag got my attention.

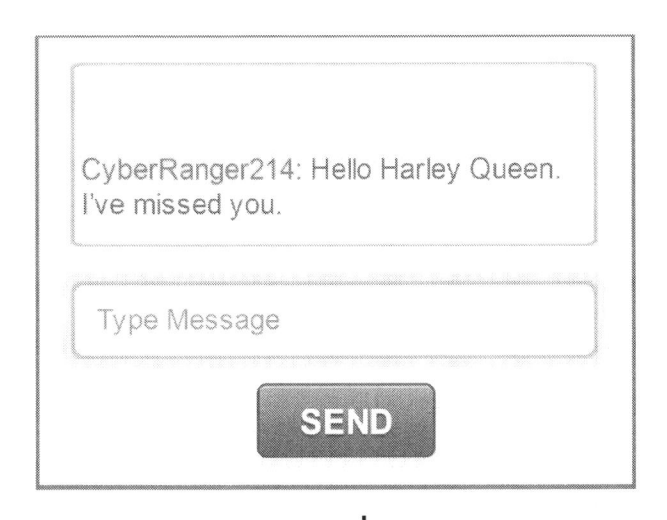

> CyberRanger214: Hello Harley Queen. I've missed you.
>
> Type Message
>
> **SEND**

My heart refused to beat and I sat staring at the message until my eyes prickled with tears. My lungs felt too heavy. The constant deep pulls of air to balance out the overwhelming fear made my vision blur and fuzz.

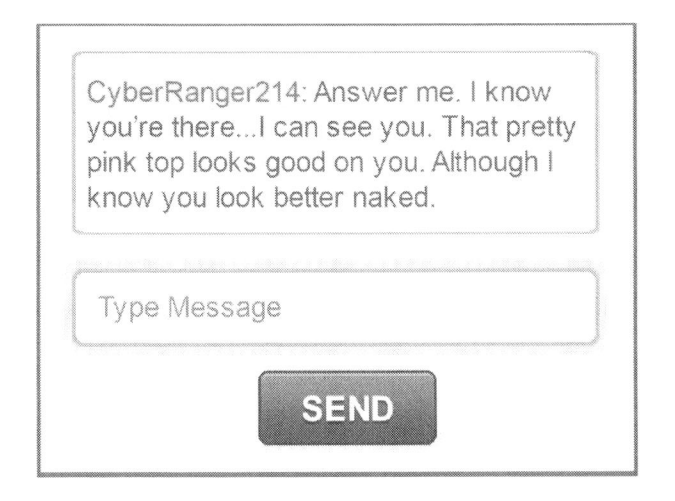

> CyberRanger214: Answer me. I know you're there...I can see you. That pretty pink top looks good on you. Although I know you look better naked.
>
> Type Message
>
> **SEND**

Blood rushed from my head into my chest and my chair shot backwards when I scrambled to move. It crashed to the floor and I tripped over it as I ran through the room to the steps.

I needed air. The door bounced off the wall when I flung it open and made a dash for the back of the house.

My throat wrestled between the air going in, and the vomit coming out. My ribs ached the harder I retched, my dry heaves bruising with a ferociousness that had me hugging my middle in attempt to ease the pain.

"Why didn't I think!" I chastised myself when Evan came up beside me. "How fucking stupid could I be?"

Knowing he'd read the message after I'd reacted so dramatically, he growled. "I'm gonna kill the fucker!"

Pulling out his phone, he contacted one of our friends whose expertise in surveillance had been useful a few times. "Need an overhaul at Harley's," he spoke sharply. "Now. We'll cover costs for your callout."

Anger raced through me like an inferno. I couldn't breathe for it. I couldn't see for the ripple of heat pouring into my vision. I couldn't stop the roar of fury that shook my body as I flew back into the house and ran down the steps to the basement.

Standing in the middle of the floor, I spun around, my arms held out by my side as I hunted for any sign of a camera.

"Come on, you fucking prick! Stop hiding and come and play."

My IM pinged and I glared at it.

> CyberRanger214: I'm impressed. My Queen finally grew a backbone.
>
> Type Message
>
> SEND

"Are you going to tell me why you're doing this?" I asked, pivoting to look at every inch of the room. "Do you honestly think you can break something you left broken a year and a half ago? I have nothing to lose, Michael."

I could almost see him smirking, that cruel sneer that he used to wear when he'd make me beg for just a little bit of Cloud making my blood heat further.

"Well? Come on. You wanted my attention and you've got it."

His silence enraged me and I flung out, swiping my arm across the desk and sending my monitor skidding into the wall, the sound of breaking glass and clattering metal filling the air. Every piece of my equipment followed, my mind at breaking point as I smashed my way through the room and annihilated everything in my way.

"Harl!" Evan came up behind me, wrapping his arms around me and lifting me off the ground.

"We're ruined!" I screamed, wrestling with my best friend as he did his best to hold me down.

"It's okay," he soothed. "I'll sort it."

"How can you sort this?" I asked, shaking my head and laughing at his stupidity. "He's been watching everything we've done. Every single little job we've done. He has everything, our clients, our codes, our software, all on fucking film!"

He blanched, reality sinking in when he finally understood, and his eyes widened in fear.

"Yeah!" I nodded spitefully. "Oh yeah."

"But that doesn't mean he will do anything with it. It's encrypted."

I laughed harder, I couldn't help it. Tears of amusement ran down my face. "Jesus, Ev! I may be the best hacker this side of London. But Michael was, and always will be, the number one of everywhere. Encryption doesn't bother him. Don't you see? He now has a full client list of every job we've done. Every fucking heist, every take. And take a guess what he will do with all that info?"

"Fuck!" he hissed, stumbling backwards.

"We're dead, Evan. Every victim of our client's will soon know exactly who hacked into their systems. Our name will be accountable for every million that's been shifted from their accounts, every secret file we've been asked to move or modify. Every code we've been asked to build will now come with a virus attached. This is it. We're dead."

I sank down to the floor. "It's over."

Eighteen
CARTER

I stared at the IM, confusion and shock making me read each word slowly and carefully.

> **Ariel15:** It's over. Thank you for everything.
>
> Type Message
>
> **SEND**

Quickly typing back before she closed down our connection, I braced myself.

> Caesar044: It's not over until the fourth is neutralised, pretty girl.
> Ariel15: I'm not sure this is even secure anymore. It's over.
> Goodbye.

> Type Message

> **SEND**

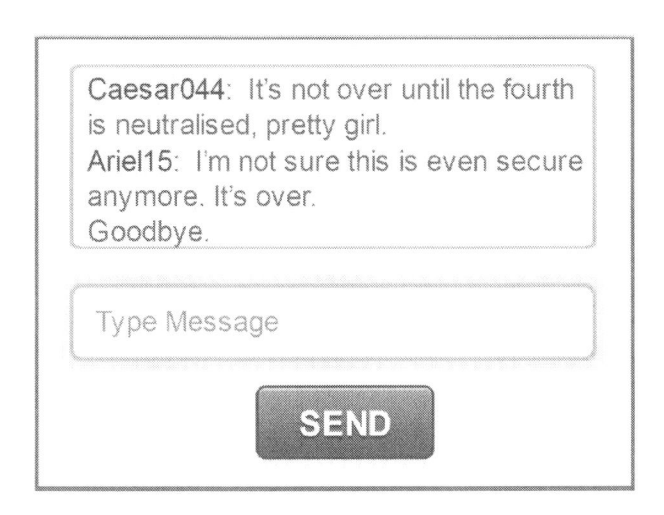

"No, no, no!" I muttered when she severed our link.

"What's up?" Jobe frowned, taking the bottle of whisky that sat next to me on the desk, filled a glass for himself and topped mine up.

"She's ended it. Something's not right."

"Why would she stop now?"

"I don't know. But I have a feeling it's something to do with Michael McKenzie."

She couldn't just decide it was over. I wouldn't let her. We were both engulfed in it, and I was just as hungry for their deaths as she was – *had been*. It didn't make sense.

Jobe suddenly sucked in a breath as he looked down at his phone. "Guess who took the bait?"

"Charlotte?"

He laughed, giving me a wink. "The one and only."

"Then let's begin Number Two."

Grinning, he gave out a quick squeal of excitement, the crazy part of him that was always trying to break its way out finding a crack in the walls he struggled to build around it. "I was hoping you'd say that."

Her wide blue eyes fixed on mine when she spotted me walking through the restaurant towards her. She jolted, unsure whether to stand or remain seated as I approached her. "Hey." She smiled and eventually decided to stand.

I remained tight-lipped, unsure of how I felt coming face to face with her again. My heart was pounding, but it wasn't with love this time. Yet, my eyes feasted on her, filling up on her beauty. "You look good, Charlotte."

"And you," she said quietly, retaking her seat as I lowered myself into the one opposite her.

She stared at me, her expression full of something I didn't want to see. "So, how have you been?"

Nodding, I grinned. "Good. Really good."

We both looked up at the waiter when he stood expectantly with his pen poised over his little notebook. "Johnnie Walker, no ice," I snapped, affronted that he couldn't even be bothered with pleasantries, his bored expression making my fist twitch.

Charlotte's eyes widened at my bluntness. The waiter quirked a brow at her, silently asking her what she wanted. She blinked and stuttered, "Oh, uhh, Merlot please."

He nodded and then disappeared, without a single word.

Shaking my head, I turned back to Charlotte. "You must be wondering why I got in touch?"

She nodded. "Yes. Especially after so long. Plus, we didn't part on…."

"That's all in the past." Reaching across the table, I took her hand and attempted to soften my gaze. My heart was beating furiously, the fever that was swamping me at the touch of her again making the room appear to spin around me. I was amazed how things had shifted. How love could mould into such a physical hatred. "The truth is, Charlotte. Well I've never really been able to move on. I said some horrible things to you, and…"

"No," she cut in. She seemed different than how she used to be. She was quieter, timid, and it surprised me. She'd always been so confident and forward, yet now she sat meekly, like she was terrified of me. She should be. She fucking should be. "I… It was on me; we both know that. What you said was justified. I was such a horrible person."

"So," I barked quickly, cutting her off abruptly. I didn't want to go on that trip with her. If she had found a conscience, then I wasn't going to be the one to stem her guilt. I wanted it to fucking drown her. "How's the family?"

She squinted in surprise at my sudden change of direction, and gave the waiter a smile of thanks when he placed her wine on the table. Taking a large mouthful, she swallowed it before addressing my question. "Mummy and Daddy have moved out to San Francisco."

"Really?" I widened my eyes with false astonishment. "Good for them. And Gareth?"

She stilled, and then winced. "Well, Gareth isn't doing so good."

"No?" Planting a fake look of concern on my face I took a gulp of whisky to disguise the smile that I was struggling to keep supressed.

"He, uhh, got into some trouble. His friends weren't good people, and they stitched him up."

I had to bite my lip to stop the bark of laughter. "Oh?"

She shook her head. "Gareth did nothing wrong, but they blamed him for everything. He's in Belmarsh, and there's not a damn thing I can do to help him. I feel so useless." Tears welled in her eyes, and if I had a conscience I would have felt a pang of pity for her. Except I didn't. I was loving every little bit of her misery.

Sighing sympathetically, I gave her hand another squeeze. "Would you like me to go and see him? I don't suppose he gets many visitors."

Her eyes widened once again. "You would do that?"

"Sure. Me and Gareth got on okay. I liked him. Anything I can do to help, babe."

"I don't know what to say," she mewed, smiling across the table at me. "I'll arrange a visiting order."

I nodded, then right on cue, my phone rang. "Yeah," I huffed into it.

Jobe chuckled at the other end. "Thought it was about time I saved you."

"I'm on my way."

Disappointment spread across Charlotte's face when I stood up. "I'm sorry. A problem I have to deal with."

She stood up and I leaned in, dropping a kiss to her cheek as I fought to contain the shudder of repulsion slicing through my gut. "I'm sorry too. It was good to see you."

Gazing at her, I ran the backs of my fingers across her prominent cheekbone, my mind only seeing the smear of tears across another beautiful woman's face. It was the only way I could stomach touching Charlotte, imaging her as another. "You'll let me know when the VO comes through?"

"Of course." She nodded eagerly, grinning up at me. "Thank you so much."

Giving her a wink, I turned and walked away, pressing the phone to my ear when I stepped outside and took in huge gulps of air. "Hook, line and fucking sinker."

Jobe laughed. "Time to play with Number Two."

"Fuck, yes. Gareth is mine."

And fuck me, when I forced his sister to watch every second of his death, only then would the hole that had been torn into my heart finally heal. I told myself that Gareth was mine for my revenge on Charlotte. But I knew, deep inside, that Charlotte had nothing to do with the reason for all the hatred bubbling up inside me. Gareth had hurt my girl – there it was again – and for that he would pay. As painfully as possible. It was just unfortunate that I wouldn't be the one to take Gareth's last breath, yet I wanted to watch the fear in his eyes when I told him I was going to make him pay for his involvement in breaking Harley Davids. I wanted to watch the realisation seep into his eyes when he knew he was going to die.

It had been easy to set up his murder, but they wouldn't, not until I had had my enjoyment with him first. And when the video came through of his torture and very painful death, Charlotte would get an anonymous copy.

And so would Harley. She thought it was over. But it was far from it.

Nineteen
HARLEY

"I'm glad you decided to relent, Harley."

My stomach roiled and saliva filled my mouth as my body prepared for purging. Bill Clancy's hand held mine with a force that was less than gentle and gave away his fears—that I would run. Believe me, I wanted to, but I knew what was good for my health. Safety. Bill was definitely not good for my health, but he would keep me physically safe, and that would do for now. I had decided to relent, but not because I'd suddenly become partial to leery politicians. I'd decided to come out with him tonight because when Michael finally revealed the aim of his game, I'd need protection I couldn't get from anywhere other than standing beside Bill Clancy MP. Sure, I knew he wouldn't be able to grant me judicial immunity, but I also knew that seeing me go to prison wouldn't be Michael's goal. He had something much worse in mind, and that would be where Bill came in.

"I figured a drink couldn't do any harm."

"Certainly not."

The backs of his fingers trailed down my arm and it took all the strength I had not to push him away. Instead, I took a healthy gulp of the white wine he'd ordered and tried to pretend it wasn't his hands on me, but those of someone else who had played with my mind in entirely different ways.

"You know," he continued, taking a leisurely sip of his own wine. "I always knew we'd be good together. I knew you'd give in."

Because I was a wealthy, intelligent woman and he was a wealthy man who knew how to feign intelligence? I had a feeling that wasn't what he meant. What he meant was, I was a woman—just a woman—and he was a powerful man; the way he saw it, I was susceptible to the charm he thought he had. I scoffed on another hard gulp.

"How so?" I asked, out of curiosity. I already knew what was going on in his little peanut-sized brain.

"Have you selected your choices?" the waiter asked when he arrived at our table.

I opened my mouth to order, but Bill took over and chose for me. Pointless me having a menu, really. I wouldn't have chosen the boeuf-whatever it was, and I certainly wouldn't have ordered oysters to start. But I'd play the good little date because when Michael came for me, I would hide behind him and pretend I knew nothing about any allegations. The mission may have failed, but my determination to keep my life—just for a while longer—hadn't gone anywhere. I don't know what else Bill and the waiter talked about, while my date spouted his creepy arse-licking bullshit and the waiter lapped up in the hopes of receiving a mighty tip; I'd zoned out and when I snapped back to reality, Bill had turned his body to shield us from the rest of the restaurant...as he poured two lines of cocaine onto a silver side-plate.

"What is this?" I asked, like I'd been reduced to one brain cell, and it had gone into self-preservation mode.

"Just a little Charlie," he said, rolling up a fifty pound note and pointing it at me. "It'll lighten the mood just a little."

"I didn't have you down as a snorter, Mr Clancy."

I took the money anyway, knowing that little line would have worn off in no time, and I could leave him riding the high while I ate and wormed my way under his wing. The cocaine was a welcome treat, and I inhaled deeply after the first hit so I could feel every single grain of my Cloud.

Bill snorted his line and I took the moment, as he relished in the bliss I knew he was no veteran at experiencing, to look at my phone. It had been buzzing constantly, and I knew exactly who it was—I'd just chosen not to answer it.

It was like the pocket money you got as a child. You knew it was in your pocket and you didn't want to touch it because you knew once you had, it would be gone. It burned a hole in my pocket, the need to talk to him, and I knew once I did, I'd be stuck—the mission would be resurrected and I'd not only be putting my life in danger, but the stranger's who had decided to help me, too.

> **Caesar044**: Hey, pretty girl. Can we talk?
>
> **Caesar044**: I know you can see this. I just want to know what happened.
>
> **Caesar044**: I don't usually do the pestering thing but...I miss you. I need to know you're okay.
>
> **Caesar044**: I'm not giving up. I told you I'd hit your targets and by God, I'll hit your targets.
>
> **Caesar044**: The ball is in your court, pretty girl, but we've got something here. I'm asking you to let me in. I'm a stranger...what harm can I do?

[Type Message]

SEND

A lot. The answer to his fifth message was a lot. The people who could harm us the most were the ones we allowed to get too close. The people who condemned us to misery and loneliness were the ones who promised us happiness and gave us hope.

> Caesar044: Please, Harley. Please let me in.
>
> Type Message
>
> SEND

Harley. He'd called me Harley. He knew who I was. How? The bastard. In one message, he told me I was safe and in the next, he was as dangerous as everyone else. I knew I shouldn't have looked at the messages.

"Harley?" A warm hand and thick fingers wrapped around my wrist and when I looked up, Bill was holding an oyster towards me. "Just open your mouth and swallow, sweetheart."

The spark of arousal in his voice told me what he was thinking and I couldn't control the retch.

"I don't like them," I said, my voice distant and vibrato.

"No?" He pursed his lips, shrugged and tipped the oyster into his mouth. "They taste of the sea."

"Never much liked the sea."

I was rambling. I was incoherent and fuzzed. Why was I talking about the sea? I wanted to go to the seaside. I wanted ice cream and to watch the boats out on the horizon.

"What did you give me?" I asked.

"Nothing you haven't had before."

He knew me. How did he know about my habit? Was I safe around anyone? Did anyone in my life *not* want to abuse and kill me?

"I..." No point in denying it now. "It's...different."

"No." Bill shook his head. "No, it's not."

He called for the waiter and everything around me moved in slow motion, my head began to loll, my eyes began to droop, and I couldn't fucking breathe. I started to gasp and choke, my breaths coming short and shallow; my fingers tingled with numbness and my vision slipped in and out.

"You're okay. You're having a panic attack."

Suddenly, Bill wasn't an asshole. He was flicking water on my face, thrusting my head between my legs, and stroking my hair away so I didn't choke on it. Suddenly, he really was helping me, when I was powerless to help myself.

"Deep breaths," he instructed, stroking his fingers down my back. He wasn't completely selfless. But he was seizing the opportunity to touch me and pass it off as help. "In through your nose, out through your mouth."

"I want..." I stopped and took a deep breath as my heart began to regulate. "I want to go home."

"Okay, we'll take you." Bill turned to the waiter and I vaguely registered a crowd of people around me, watching me flake. "Have my car brought around."

"Yes, sir."

Bill helped me stand and after throwing my arm over his shoulder to support myself, he wrapped his arm around my waist, sliding lower with every shaky step I took. He was an asshole, and I wanted to turn and ask for someone to help, tell someone I didn't think I'd be getting the ride home I wanted, but who could I trust? Who was watching me and who had been brought into this sick joke that was my life?

Bill eased me into the car and slid into the back seat next to me. No sooner had I plugged my seatbelt in, I was being woken up by strong arms holding me and pulling me from the car.

The scent was familiar. The route we were taking felt familiar, like I did it every day. Because I did. I was outside my house.

"Please," I whispered, full consciousness finding me as I looked up.

Two eyes met mine, but even in the darkness I could see their uniqueness. I could see the contrast in colour and the stark shade of ice and jade I'd only ever seen in one man before.

"Carter..."

"It's okay, Harley. I've got you."

I wanted to squirm away from him, to ask him how and why he'd betrayed my trust. But I wanted to hug him. I wanted to hold him and I wanted him to hold me back, because he'd broken through barriers I'd been reinforcing for years and, finally, the ordeal I'd suffered for my addiction had been rewritten by pleasure and excitement.

"I'm sorry," I said as he walked me up the steps to the front of the house. "I shouldn't have bailed like that."

He laughed, his chuckle deep and throaty. It brought a sheet of goose bumps to the surface of my skin and I sighed in contentment.

"Where's Bill?"

"I was here waiting for you. I told him I'd take you to bed." He took a deep breath and reached the front door. "So you told him we broke up, huh? Is that what we did?"

"You said it yourself, don't overthink it."

Carter set me down and I held onto the hanging basket beside the front door for support as he fished in my bag for my keys and let us in. The door opened and the darkness of my home seeped out.

"You should leave a light on when you're not home."

I flung my arm out to stop him going into the house when he raised his foot and moved to enter.

"I do."

I pushed past him, forcing my way into the hallway and switching the light on. I slipped on a wet patch just inside the front door and fell backwards. Carter caught me, but the damage had been done. He didn't need to grip the tops of my arms and force me to turn to face him. He didn't need to tug me into him and hold me in a death grip as my knees buckled. He didn't need to turn the light back off and pull me from the house.

I'd seen it.

"Let me go!" I screamed, pushing at his chest until his arms fell away.

I turned and crumbled to the floor on my hands and knees, crawling across the floor, through the blood soaked into my carpet, until I stopped in front of Evan's body and fell to the floor next to him. His eyes were open, fixed on me although they held no focus. Blood matted my hair, soaked into my clothes and seeped from my heart as it broke for my best friend. My brother. The second brother to be taken from me. A wail escaped me and sobs soon followed, until my head thumped, my eyes ran dry, and every muscle in my body ached. But I didn't stop.

Twenty
CARTER

I'd seen death a hundred times. I'd created it more times than I could count.

I'd never been as devastated by it as when I stood by the front door and watched my girl—yes, *my* girl—break. The death of her friend had been no accident. He'd been murdered, and the knife used to do it had been left in his neck. Evan—Harley said it a hundred times over the course of the night—had got caught up in this shit storm and he'd paid with his life. As I watched Harley crumble before she curled in on herself and bathed in his blood as she clung to his lifeless body, I felt something I hadn't felt in a long, *long* time.

Guilt.

Ending the trouble my girl had found herself in had been my job. If I had done the it, finished what she'd started while keeping her and everyone around her safe, Evan wouldn't be dead, and we wouldn't be stuck in the conundrum of what the fuck we were supposed to do now.

"Harley, babe," I whispered, approaching her cautiously and placing my hands on her icy shoulders. "Let me give you a shower."

She shook her head, but she didn't have the strength to fight me off as the grief became her...and then became me. I could no longer hide inside my shell. She'd cracked through it. She'd cracked my code; whatever the fuck she'd done to me, she'd won. I had a niggling thought in the back of my mind, as I carried her upstairs and into the bathroom, that this had something to do with the hit on her. I knew I was supposed to kill her; I'd accepted money to do it and devoted the past few weeks of my life to keeping her safe, but someone wanted her dead. Had that someone turned up tonight and found Evan instead?

I turned on the shower and sat her on the toilet as I stripped her clothes from her. She was catatonic, staring through me as if I wasn't there, but I persevered. If this was my fault, I had to find a way to fix it. When her clothes were in a pile on the bathroom floor, I lifted her into the cubicle. She stood still, leaning against the tiles and looking down like Evan was lying in front of her. I took my clothes off and joined her, instantly taking her in my arms and holding her tight as the hot water poured over us.

"We were kids when we met," she said, her voice monotonous and dry. "He's been with me through it all. He stood by my side when my family died, and he's been there ever since. What am I supposed to do without him?" She keened quietly, snuggling into me as another sob ripped from her and tore me in half. "I need him. I can't do this without him!"

"We'll find who did this," I promised, combing my hands through her hair. "I swear to God, Harley, we'll find who did this and make them pay."

She nodded, but didn't believe me. I knew, if I was ever going to redeem myself, I had to take the first step now. I had to forge a connection between us—one we'd had for weeks since before we met at her gallery.

"Julius Caesar was killed by a man called Marcus Brutus in the year 44BC. A hitman using the name Brutus would have raised flags, so the victim became the cover. Caesar became a mask."

"Caesar?" she asked, stilling against me as reality slammed into her. "44?"

"Yes, pretty girl. I'm Caesar044."

She fell to her knees and I let her, moving with her so she was cradled on my lap. I thought she'd push me away, but she didn't. I thought she'd break down, but she held strong.

"You..." I nodded as she stumbled over her words. "You're a hitman."

I shook my head. That wasn't important. I had never discussed my job—I had never told anyone on this planet what I did and I wasn't about to disclose information now—it didn't matter. What mattered was now she could believe me. She would know, without doubt, that I would find these cunts and end them, and she was safer with me than she would be with anyone else.

"I'm the man who's going to finish your list and find the person who murdered your friend, Harley."

"But you...you kill people."

"Don't act so shocked now. You hired a hitman. You figured he was fucking someone, you just didn't assume it would be you."

"But..."

She froze and I felt the tension smother her as the water continued to batter our naked bodies, and the connection we'd kept separate, between real life and virtual life, forged into one almighty connection that stole my breath. It had been a long, *long* time since I'd held someone, and I didn't want to let Harley Davids go. Ever.

She seemed to agree, as she sat up, wrapped her arms around my neck and fused her lips to mine. She tasted of sorrow and devastation, but it was a powerful fucking aphrodisiac that had my cock springing to attention and nudging the lips of her pussy as she straddled me.

"Jesus, Harley," I groaned into her mouth as she rolled her hips, stroking her beautiful cunt along the length of my shaft. "I haven't got anything."

"I don't care," she muttered, trailing her tongue over my top lip. "Tell me you're clean, and then make me clean...take it all away."

I growled and fisted her hair. I didn't deal well with women demanding shit from me, and I wouldn't start now. She'd pushed me far enough and while I wanted to be soft, I wanted to fuck her until she forgot every one of her problems. She gasped when I pulled her head back and dived into her neck, my other hand squeezing her firm tit and scraping my fingernail over her nipple. She shuddered, and moaned. I gripped her hips and heard her breath hitch with anticipation. When I impaled her, she threw her head back and cried out.

"I can make you forget, babe." I slammed up into her and stilled when a spear of pleasure surged up my spine. "Forgetting is what I do best, but-" I thought for a second, wondering if I wanted to invest this much of myself. When she lowered herself onto me, taking every fucking inch, she made my decision for me. I wouldn't be without her. "we're going to deal with this. We're going to sort your shit out."

"Okay," she moaned.

"I mean it." Leaning back so I was resting on the wall of the shower, I lifted her higher so I could spank her. "I mean it, Harley."

"Okay!" She screamed, fisting my hair and pulling hard. "Just shut up now. Do this later."

That was a command I would follow. No more talking. Instead, I drove up into her and slammed her body down onto me until she was tightening around me, her legs quivering, voice breaking with her cries that soon turned to sobs of grief and paralysing pleasure. She came, squeezing me like a fucking vice and dragging my own orgasm out. I spilled into her, feeling my warmth hit hers and collide in a cocktail of regret and the urge to do it again and again and again. I kept her pressed to me, softening inside her as I hugged her close and we floated down from the high.

"I'm sorry," she said, sliding off me with a shiver that made me race to my feet and turn the shower off. "I shouldn't have done that."

"Shut up, Harley."

I climbed out of the cubicle, wrapped a towel around me and held one open for her. She stepped out after me, accepted it, and then—surprisingly—she accepted the hug I offered her. We both stood dripping in the middle of her bathroom, refusing to break this connection because reality was a fucking prick, and karma had it in for us.

Harley hadn't slept. She'd made me give up my old t-shirt and she sat in it all night, while I sat in my boxers next to her. I made her coffee—she didn't touch it. I made her tea—she didn't drink it. She sat on the sofa in front of the TV and watched the news. We watched the sunrise in Japan and Australia, and watched the stock market positions and predictions for the day. We watched replay after replay of latest news, sports news, celebrity gossip, and weather forecasts, and Harley refused to move. After our shower, she'd returned to her frozen state—a state I desperately wanted to crack. By 10am, we'd been in the same place for almost twelve hours, with a dead body a few feet behind us, and a million unasked and unanswered questions swimming around us.

Until the news channel hit with a news report.
Fuck.

"Good morning. I'm Kelley Scott, reporting for Sky News Breakfast." A red banner slid across the bottom of the screen, brandishing bold white letters that read: BREAKING NEWS. "Breaking news this morning. Bill Clancy, a valued and respected member of the conservative party has died at the age of fifty-six. Emergency services were called to an address in the capital last night amidst rumours the MP had collapsed at his home after returning from a night out. Paramedics treated him on the scene and he was taken to a nearby hospital, but it is reported that he passed away sometime after six o'clock this morning. Sky News will bring you all the updates as the story unfolds."

"Carter…"

When I looked at Harley, she was glaring at me with fear in her deep brown eyes. Her catatonia had broken and she was shaking, trembling, her fists clenched on her lap as she stared wide-eyed at me.

"Yes?"

"Did you do this?"

I seethed, my nostrils flaring. "Am I going to be accused every time some fucker dies? How could I have killed the cunt? I was here with you."

I waited for her to calm, for her anger and suspicion to soothe, while my inner-asshole laughed like a hyena inviting the vultures to play.

Of course I'd fucking killed him.

"You're lying."

She stood up, momentarily stunned when she looked towards the front door where Evan laid. I stayed still as she strode across the room towards me and jumped onto my lap, her knees either side of my thighs.

"You killed him, I know you did. You were the last person to see him alive and an *assassin* wouldn't leave a trail. So you stayed with me. Why did you kill him?"

I chewed on my bottom lip and cursed these bullshit feelings I had for this chick. Why couldn't I just smack her, watch her tumble off me, and then get the fuck out with my safety intact? She was too fucking close. Too. Fucking. Close.

"You think I didn't see him slip you the cocaine?" I asked, watching her eyes bulge with shock. "You think I didn't see him raping you with his eyes? Touching you? Touching what's mine? He gave you drugs, Harley. Sure, he helped you when your anxiety moved in, but the cunt was going to rape you. Pricks like him aren't worth the air they breathe."

"So you *killed* him?" she shrieked, slapping my cheek, then the other. My skin burned, but I'd give her those for free. "You can't just go around killing people!"

"No? Does that include Gareth Johnson?"

"Don't fucking mention their names," she growled, pressing her hands to my shoulders and squeezing. "It's different."

"Is it?" I cocked a brow. "So you can hire me to kill them because they hurt you, but *I* can't kill a man who hurts you."

"You…" she stopped, then backtracked. "You did it to protect me?"

"Of course."

"Why?"

Pushing her off me, I stood up. "I don't fucking know. I don't want to fucking know. All I know is,

I'm breaking all my rules for you, and I don't regret a single deviation."

"Carter…"

"Don't." I raised my hand and took a step back. "I told you not to overthink it. I'm here, and I'm not going anywhere. I'll kill to keep you safe and that isn't going to change anytime soon, so get used to it. And I am who I am…again, that isn't going to change. I don't care if you learn to tolerate it or not—you're mine, Harley, and I protect what's mine."

Twenty-one

HARLEY

"I need to... take care of Evan," Carter said softly, placing a kiss to the tip of my nose before he lifted me from his knee and placed me on the sofa.

I stared up at him, his words not making sense. "What?"

"His body." The gentility from moments ago had already faded, leaving a stark coldness in his eyes. "We can't leave him there."

Shaking my head, I kept my gaze on his face, refusing to even glance behind me at Evan's body. Carter was right, of course; we couldn't very well leave him laid out in my hallway, but my heart wouldn't accept what Carter was trying to do. "No."

He sighed, tipping his head. "So you want to call the police?"

Fear made me suck air through clenched teeth. "I... They can't come here." My thoughts moved to my basement. Evan had been murdered in my house. The police would be all over it with a fine-toothcomb, my secrets out in the open for all the damn world to see.

Now it all made sense and rage made my teeth crack when my jaw clenched hard. "Oh, you clever boy!" I whispered to myself, but Carter caught my fury.

"What aren't you telling me, Harley?"

"Michael," I seethed, closing my eyes and groaning. "He knew what this would bring out into the open."

"Michael McKenzie?"

I stilled, lifting my eyes to Carter and narrowing them. "Just how much do you know?"

"That he's your Number Four." He was so blasé about knowing my life that my head shook.

Did he know about my Cloud addiction?

He came to crouch in front of me and took my hands. "What did he do? I know he had something to do with the scars on your chest. Did he do them? Was he the one who marked you?"

"I have to phone Ben."

Anger flashed in Carter's remarkable eyes, the colours swirling like a night-storm. "I will find out, babe. From you, or from Michael himself. It doesn't matter which, but I will find out."

Pushing him away I reached for my bag, pulling out my phone. Ben's name mocked me, my hands shaking and hindering me from hitting the icon to call him.

Carter took the phone from me and pressed 'call.' I watched him, tears spilling onto my cheeks when he gently informed Benny that his best friend was dead. The sound of his tortured cry through the phone made my heart split open and spill grief into the oxygen around me. The air seemed too thick with the potency of it, making it difficult to draw a breath.

I ran from the room, leaving Carter talking quietly to Ben, and hurriedly dug out my stash.

After slamming the bathroom door behind me and making sure to lock it, I scrambled to form four lines, my mouth watering at the sight of such simplistic perfection. My mind wanted out. My heart wanted to stop hurting. And my soul danced with an eagerness when I inserted the straw up my left nostril and inhaled sharply and deeply.

Moving down, I snorted the next line, hungry for a quick hit.

My mind buzzed, my heartrate slowed and the burning scorch of the blood in my veins cooled after line number three. Sliding down, I hastily sucked up the last line and closed my eyes when oblivion caressed the suffering inside me, the high forcing me to ride on a wave of tranquillity.

It wasn't until the sound of splintering wood, and Carter's animalistic growl filled my ears, that my eyes slowly slid back open.

His words were slurred as fingers tightened around my arms and my body was hauled through the upper floor of my home. "You're a fucking junkie!" he seethed to himself, mumbling words I couldn't distinguish through the high as he flung me on the bed. "You stupid, stupid fucking girl."

I laughed, his voice travelling into my brain alongside the hum of ecstasy. "Yeah, Carter," I slurred, forcing my eyes open to watch the fury on his face. "Yeah, I'm a filthy druggie. I'm a whore. Did you not know? Michael made sure anyone after him knew that. What the fuck, Carter. It's displayed on my chest in plain fucking English."

His hand tightened around my throat but the haze ruling me vetoed any fear I should have felt. "How long?"

I laughed again, my head falling to the side.

Carter fisted my hair, pulling my face back to his. "How fucking long, Harley?"

"I thought you knew all about me, Carter? I thought you knew every aspect of my sad fucking life when you got your friend to fuck me."

Shock covered his face and he even had the gall to look guilty.

"Oh." I laughed. "Did you think I didn't know? You think I'm such a whore that I wouldn't even realise that it was two different men fucking me? Especially after having three men fuck every single fucking hole on my body. You think I wouldn't know?" I screamed the last bit, tears of horror and self-hatred tearing at my chest and forcing the confined sob in my heart free.

"Shit!" He fisted his hair and spun around, refusing me to see when realisation exploded across his face.

"What the fuck?"

Ben's voice had me reaching out blindly. Immediately his hand found mine and he pulled me into his chest. "I'm here, Harl. I'm here!"

"Benny!" I cried, clinging to him as devastation crippled me. "Evan, Ben. Evan!"

"I know, sweetheart," he choked out, the grief in his voice attaching itself to mine and making it impossible to breathe.

"I want it to go away, Ben."

He nodded, his chin rubbing across the top of my head. "How much have you had?"

"Just four," I pleaded with my eyes as I looked up at him in expectation.

He shook his head and sighed, "No more, not yet."

"You fucking condone this… this shit?" Carter barked.

I'd forgotten about him as my friend's arms encompassed my pain. Ben tensed, his hold on me tightening when he looked up at Carter. "Not now, mate."

"Not now?" Carter scoffed, shaking his head roughly. "Then fucking when? She's your friend, and you allowed her to get in this mess!"

Ben was up so fast my body fell back onto the bed. Carter's back slammed against the wall with Ben's fury. "You think I did this to her? You think I can take her fucking pain away? I didn't do this! Michael did!"

Carter's eyes snapped my way, and I closed my own so I wouldn't have to see the shock looking back at me.

"Michael used her. And he made damn sure that Harley would use him. He supplied her, he used her, and he fucked her up in a way none of us could ever comprehend. You have no idea what goes inside her head, and if fucking coke takes away her nightmares, then I'll sell my soul to supply her myself."

Carter mumbled another 'fuck' before he stormed from the room, the loud bang of the door making me wince. Every part of me ached with self-hatred, my tears punishing me as they burnt my eyes and scorched my skin.

"It's okay, sweetheart," Ben soothed, sliding me into his arms again. "I'll sort it. I promise, Harl. I promise."

I nodded, allowing his words to ease the agony inside. Ben would sort it. My friend would make it all okay again.

Yet, when my eyes shifted to the door Carter had just left through, I had a feeling there would be nothing left for Ben to fix.

Twenty-two
CARTER

Gareth looked confused when he finally walked into the visiting area and his eyes settled on mine. I could see the hint of fear nestled in those pretty blues and I couldn't hide the slow grin that crept across my face. The cunt had been kept waiting, held back until visiting time was nearly over. It was easier to hide the pause on the surveillance camera that way, only ten minutes to cover up instead of thirty.

Gareth and I had always had an okay relationship, so the unease etched on his pretty-boy face told me there was already a whisper on the block. But I had sat back, crossed my arms over my chest and used the low murmur of other conversation to keep me entertained until he arrived. Whispers become ears-splitting when they're the truth and I'd needed to keep a low profile.

"Gareth." I looked at him when he slid his long, thin body into the hard, plastic chair opposite me.

"Well, well, well." He narrowed his eyes on me. "When Charlotte said you wanted to visit, I thought she'd finally lost it."

"Your sister lost it a long time ago."

He blinked in shock, but then shrugged and nodded in agreement. "Yeah. Well, our Lottie was always a bit of a slapper when it came to men." His words were meant to offend me. He didn't know me very well. It told me more about him, that speaking of his sister so derogatorily just proved he was no longer an asset to this planet. Blood was blood at the end of the day, and if you didn't stick up for your kin, then what the fuck was left in life?

"Men with money," I corrected, my anger already on edge. I wanted to yank the motherfucker across the table by his face and rip his throat out in front of all the pricks daring to look our way.

A buzzer sounded and Gareth's face lit up. "Shit, so soon? Well thanks for the quick visit."

I chuckled as various chairs scraped across the floor, the noise almost deafening as the other inmates piled out and Gareth stood up.

Tutting at him, and shaking my head, I grinned and stood up. Before his feet even moved, my hand captured the back of his head and I slammed his face into the table. "Not so fast, Gareth. I haven't finished."

I glanced up at Bob, the 'very friendly after a couple of ton hit his palm' PO, when he gave me a sharp nod and turned to leave, pulling the door closed behind him.

"What the fuck?" Gareth spat, squirming beneath my hold but getting nowhere.

"It appears I have more friends than you, Gareth. There's a surprise."

His eyes glared up at me, his cheek spread out over the table with the force of my grasp. "What do you want?"

I laughed, excitement bubbling through me. "Now, let's see. Firstly, take a deep breath, you fucking prick, because there won't be many more."

He looked confused for a moment. "You're doing this because of what Charlotte did to you and Jobe?"

"I'm doing this for Harley Davids!" I roared, sheer revulsion trickling inside me with the images in my head. I had to grit my teeth for strength when Harley's blood and tear-streaked face found the front of my mind; three men using her, abusing her, and marking her for life. "I am doing this because I can. Because you crossed a line when you touched my girl."

"Your girl?" Fear clouded his eyes and seeped from his filthy body, marbling the air around me as my own rage ignited every molecule of oxygen. "But she was Mikey's girl."

"She was never Mikey's girl," I spat, crushing his windpipe beneath the heel of my hand. His eyes bulged and I relished in the sound of bone splintering with the power of my wrath.

Forcing myself to ease back when he screamed and Bob appeared at the door in a warning, I bent down and spat in his ear. "Take a breath, Gareth. Take a long, *long* breath."

He spluttered when I let him go and turned to walk away. "And enjoy it," I told him quietly when Bob came to escort him out of the room. I watched as he guided him around the corner into the small cell with three men waiting to earn their pay.

Forty minutes later an unused email I had created specifically for the occasion pinged with the arrival of a video.
And I smiled.
Two down, two to go.

Twenty-three
HARLEY

It had been over ten days since Carter had left, and Evan had died. My soul was void of anything. I didn't feel, I didn't eat, I didn't live. I just existed on coffee and Cloud. And I only existed to find Number Three.

The house had been overhauled by Evan's friend, his expertise at surveillance uncovering four microscopic recording devices. I felt safe, strangely. It was like Evan lived in the basement with me, his encouragement, his love and his need for revenge spurring me on. I was alone now, apart from Ben. But Carter, or Caesar, was gone, and Evan's death had given me back the fight to find Michael and end this once and for all.

Never-ending files, mind-numbing codes, unbreakable hash-codes, torturous proto-sweeps, and endless amounts of coffee finally paid off when on the following Sunday afternoon, a quiet alarm woke me from my dozing.

My heart physically gasped when a name blinked on my monitor. Sucking in a fortifying breath, I plugged into the national security database and input the name. A face instantly shook my core.

"BEN!" I shouted as a chill raced up my spine and exploded into my brain. "BEN!"

He came scrambling down the stairs, a fresh cup of coffee he had made spilling across the floor as he scurried up beside me.

"Well, fuck me." He looked at me, a huge fucking grin on his face as tears prickled his eyes. "You did it, Harl. You found Number Three."

I nodded, my body shaking with sheer adrenaline. No longer was I scared and tortured by the face staring at me from the screen. Now all that filled me was determination, hatred and a pure, undiluted need for carnage and destruction.

Number Three had proven to be the hardest. Only because we already knew who Number Four was. Closing my eyes, I sent a silent prayer of thanks to my friend. "Thank you, Ev," I whispered.

Turning to Ben, I chewed on my lip. "You should know," I said quietly. "Michael is mine."

His eyes widened on me. "What?"

"For Evan. Not for me." I shook my head. "My scars show I'm alive, Ben. Evan doesn't have any scars. They didn't leave him with any. Only another one in my soul. That's the last one Michael will ever put upon me."

"And Caesar?"

"Caesar is no more."

Ben narrowed his eyes on me but said no more when I stood and stretched my back.

Snatching a piece of paper from the pad, I scribbled down the details I needed.

Number Three would prove to be difficult, but only because he was out of reach to me. But not to Caesar.

Michael knew I was working my way through the other three before I got to him. Yet, I had to wonder if he knew about Caesar. For some reason I thought not. He hadn't expected Carter's expertise in shifting dead bodies. Michael had thought I'd immediately call the police, then my work den would be uncovered. But after Carter had stormed from my house, Evan had also disappeared. It hurt me that I hadn't a clue what he had done with my best friend. I wanted to mourn him, to go and say goodbye, yet it was still too raw and agonising. So I would question Carter when I knew I was more capable of coping with Evan's death.

"Where are you going?" Ben asked, watching me warily when he picked up a sulking Plum from Evan's chair where she refused to leave.

"I need Carter to take care of Number Three."

Ben stalled, his eyes probing. "What? I thought..."

"I need time." I couldn't tell Benny why, he wouldn't understand. But if Carter went after Number Three, Michael would still think he was safe. He wouldn't expect me to go after him until Number Three was dead. So what better opportunity than to take down the last two at the same time. Carter wouldn't allow me to deal with Michael myself – although maybe now he knew what I was he no longer cared. Whether he cared or not, he'd promised me he'd help me finish this...if he thought we were still on Number Three he wouldn't suspect what I was going to do.

"Harley? Time for what?"

"Number Three is Michael's right hand man. Number Three is Mole." My eyes moved to the screen. Jamie Forester's alias name, Mole, had shocked me more than anything. Mole was notorious in the underground cyber world. He was named Mole because he lived underground. He never came out, and he would prove to be impossible to get to. However, I prayed Carter had his contacts and could ferret him out.

"That's impossible." Ben shook his head, fixing his stare on the screen. "He's never been seen in public."

I laughed, a shiver racing around me when I remembered the feel of Jamie Forester's fingers in my throat and his dirty cock inside me. "We both know that's not true. I should feel honoured that I was worth a day trip out."

Ben scowled at me, grumbling under his breath at my sarcasm. "I don't like this, Harl. Something seems off."

I rolled my eyes at his worry but didn't answer him.

Shoving the paper into my back pocket, I reached up and kissed his cheek, cherishing the feel of my best friend for the last time. Slipping my arms around him, I hugged him tight. "Get the beers in. Tonight we need to get drunk."

He smiled, relief that I was finally escaping the confines of the basement making his shoulders relax. "Good girl."

I turned, quickly hiding the anxiety at what was to come, and blew out a breath.

It was time. And God help me, I would end it one way or another.

The doorman to Carter's apartment recognised me immediately. He gave me a wide smile. "Good evening, Miss."

"Hello again," I returned his smile with a tense one, my nerves on edge at seeing Carter again after what happened. "Can I go up?"

His whole body clenched and his smile dropped. He appeared to be thinking about it and I frowned. He knew who I was now, so surely he didn't need to verify my visit.

"Is there a problem?"

He glanced at the door to the elevator and clicked his tongue. "He has *company* at the moment." The way he said 'company' had my chest squeezing tight, the crushing feeling one I was not used to.

"Oh."

He grimaced, giving me a sympathetic look. "You can wait if you'd…"

"No." I shook my head, trying to make my legs work and carry me out of there. Heat blushed my cheeks with embarrassment and I moved my eyes anywhere but at the doorman who was kind enough to show me pity. I didn't want his pity. I had stupidly thought that Carter and myself had formed some sort of relationship. How could I be so stupid? I was just sex to him. Why on earth would he not take on other lovers?

I spun around, scrambling to make my brain work and figure out what to do next. My body ached with hurt and I sank my teeth into my bottom lip, the bite of pain finally slicing through my wounded pride and giving me the ability to move.

"Can I call you a cab?" the doorman offered, his voice low behind me and making me jump.

"Uhh, no, that's okay."

"Are you sure? I'm not sure I like you being out alone at this time of night."

Well at least someone cared. "I'm fine." I nodded, more to tell myself that than him.

The piece of paper in my back pocket was burning a hole through me and I turned back around. I had burned the online connection Caesar and I had previously had, so there was no way of sending him the information anymore. Only in physical form. "Actually, do you have an envelope?"

He looked surprised but then shrugged and nodded. "Sure. Hang on."

I stood, tapping my foot and examining every inch of the foyer as partygoers came and disappeared into the club, some making me jump when the doors flew open and laughter or drunken shouts spilled out, the beat of the music furthering the headache I had coming on.

The doorman reappeared and handed me an envelope. Praying I could trust him, but somehow knowing Carter wouldn't just employ anyone he hadn't already vetted, I slipped the paper in and sealed it.

"It's important that he gets this."

He smiled and nodded. "Confidentially, of course."

I liked this guy already. "Yes. Thank you so much."

"No problem, Miss. Go steady."

Fresh air hit me as soon as I stepped back into the street. It was a busy night, many revellers strolling the streets and the smell of fried food made my stomach rumble. Although I wasn't sure my nervous stomach could withstand anything other than manmade stimulation.

Taking out my phone, I opened the connection I had established after Michael had hacked into my private IM. He had obviously forgotten he'd taught me well. But then again, he had probably known I would track him. It could all be a trap. Except, I didn't care anymore.

He wanted me. And that's exactly what he would get. Me.

Twenty-four
CARTER

Charlotte stood in my doorway, her red-rimmed eyes delighting me more than they should have. Revenge was so fucking sweet. Her devastation thrilled every part of me, from the memories to the present, from the past to the sight of redemption so easily obtained.

"Charlotte?"

She shook her head, tears dripping off her cheeks and dropping onto her exposed chest. Jesus, even in grief she had to flaunt her fucking assets. "I didn't know where else to go." It actually disgusted me that she'd come straight here. Three years and I hadn't made one single effort to contact her. Then after just one meeting she'd had the nerve to come straight to me.

"Sure. Come in." I moved aside, the scent of her regular perfume making my gut twist.

She squeezed past me even though I had left her enough room to pass without touching, and she made sure to graze her tits against me as she stepped inside.

"Drink?"

She nodded, already making herself comfy on my sofa. "Please. Something strong. Do you still drink Johnnie?"

I nodded and turned my back on her to head into the kitchen. The sound of her sharp intake of breath curved a smile on my lips.

"Jobe?" Her voice was trembling, her shock evident.

"Hello, Charlotte."

I left them to reacquaint themselves as I poured three glasses. The last time all three of us had been in the same room together, things had been said, and actions had been set into motion. Actions that Jobe and I would never falter from. Our code had been etched into our souls that day, the day we began a protocol that would forever change our lives.

"So," I chirped happily as I placed the three glasses onto the table. "All of us together again. How awesome."

Charlotte's wide eyes shot to mine. She hadn't missed the sarcasm, and realising her stupidity at coming here tonight, she snatched up her glass and downed the contents in one fluid swallow.

Jobe leaned back into the sofa and chuckled. "Who'd have thought. Me, you and him, all together again."

She shifted uncomfortably. "I thought, I thought that you wouldn't..."

"We wouldn't what, Charlotte?" Jobe asked, a chill in his voice that didn't go unnoticed by either of us. "You thought you could drive a wedge between us. You really didn't know us that well, did you?"

"I..." She shook her head again, and then groaned. "I need your help."

Jobe glanced at me before turning to Charlotte. "Oh?"

She picked up her glass again and tipped it high, her tongue flicking out to catch the last dribble of whisky. She looked at me expectantly, as if I was going to top her up. I smiled and sat back into the chair. "Go on."

She scraped at her fingernails and stared at the floor. "Gareth," she said quietly. "H-he was murdered."

Both Jobe and I gasped in mock surprise. "Oh no, how awful."

Charlotte, catching the derision in Jobe's tone, frowned, but she was too stupid to work it out. Then again, she always had been. "Uhh, he left a lot of…"

"Debt?" I finished for her. Stupid, stupid bitch. Did she think I didn't know that?

She nodded, picking harder at the skin beside her perfectly manicured nails. "Yes. And now, now they'll…"

"Make you pay?" Jobe asked, leaning forwards and resting his elbows on his knees. "Oh, Charlotte." He sighed, shaking his head and giving her a pitying look.

Looking at me, she ran her tongue over her bottom lip. Used to work once. Not anymore. "I wondered if…"

I quirked an eyebrow and shook my head, pretending I didn't know what the fuck she was on about.

"I wondered if you could, you know, help me out."

"Help you out?" Jobe asked innocently. "Not sure I follow, babe."

She swung her arm out. "This place must be doing good. It's the best club in London. All my friends come here, and…. And…"

"And you thought we'd have the spare cash to pay your brother's bills?"

She tensed but nodded. "Well, yeah. I wouldn't usually ask but…."

"Yes, you would. You really would, Charlotte."

"I don't know who else to turn to," she screeched suddenly.

"Are there no others that you're playing against each other at the moment?"

She froze, her jaw dropping with Jobe's taunt. Words seemed to fail her as her mouth opened and closed but nothing came out. Eventually scrambling to her feet, she grabbed her bag off the floor. "I'm sorry, this wasn't a good idea."

"No." I gave her a wink. "No, it really wasn't, babe. You can see yourself out, huh?"

Her face blanched at my amused expression. She really thought that Jobe and I would come to her rescue, after playing us both so well?

"Hope you find the eighty K!" I shouted, just before the door slammed. The daft fuck hadn't even realised I knew exactly how much her brother actually owed.

Jobe leaned back and spread his arms over the back of the sofa, his eyes alight with glee. "Stupid fucking bitch!"

"Does revenge always taste this sweet?" I asked, shaking my head and laughing.

Jobe groaned when a knock at the door echoed through the apartment. "Oh, God. That didn't take her long."

I rolled my eyes and sighed as I opened the door, but stilled in surprise when Alec stood with a frown on his face. He handed me an envelope. "Young lady was adamant you got this. I have a feeling it's important so I brought it straight up."

I nodded, taking it from him and thanking him as I closed the door and tore the envelope open.

My eyes flew over the small piece of paper, my heart fighting to gallop and stop simultaneously. "No."

Jobe frowned, coming to stand beside me and read the note over my shoulder. "Shit. Fuck," he choked out when his eyes landed on the name. The same name that had been handed to me not an hour ago, the same name that had hired me to take out Harley Davids. The same name Harley now handed to me as her Number Three.

"Fuck!" Jobe hissed, snatching up his jacket and following me out of the apartment.

I stopped him, grabbing his wrist. "You sure you're ready to do this?"

"Never more sure." He fixed me with a stare that told me he wasn't lying. "She needs to know. She needs to know."

I nodded. My heart didn't quite agree with him. This would change everything. Everything. Yet, thought didn't even come into it. Harley had uncovered Number Three. Mole. The most notorious of the underground hackers. And if he knew she'd discovered who he was, then there was no doubt he would be more than eager to stop her running her mouth.

Twenty-five
HARLEY

Plum smelled the Chinese as soon as I closed the front door behind me and came racing around the corner, her loud mews giving me a much needed smile. "Hungry, puss?"

She purred louder, stroking the top of her head over my leg before pressing her nose to the white bag in my hand.

"Jesus, I swear Evan lives inside you." I laughed at her 'grabby hands', remembering when Evan would do the same. He would have already been snatching the bag out of my hand and diving into each plastic container.

Grabbing a bottle of wine out of the fridge, I sat Plum on the table and shared out the food.

"You know," I said to her as I watched her shovel down every piece of chicken before she even contemplated the vegetables. "You'll get acid reflux eating like that."

Her severe green eyes lifted at my voice and I swear she flipped me off with a look.

I laughed, scooping up my own chicken and loading her plate back up. I wasn't really that hungry, and I leaned back, drinking the wine as I watched my cat demolish my dinner.

Staring at my phone, I growled in frustration again. It had been two hours since I'd contacted

Michael. But nothing. I knew he was playing me, making me work for him. I just wanted it to be over now. Carter would take care of Number Three, and Number Four was mine. Except it wasn't going as I thought it would.

Grabbing the bottle and my glass I left Plum to finish off as I opened the basement door. Pushing the stump across to hold the door open for Plum to join me when she'd finished, I stepped down. The lights flicked on with my descent, the room brightening a little more the further in I got.

My kit fired up, activating Spotify as music started to hum through the various speakers around the room, and I sighed as I looked over at Evan's desk when one of his favourite tunes filled the silence. I couldn't find it within me to break his shit up yet. I frowned; there was something different, yet I couldn't put my finger on it. His desk was still exact. Evan had OCD, his desk had to be to his spec at all times, things placed in their correct space and his litter bin no higher than halfway before he would empty it.

I froze.

There it was. Sat precisely in the centre of his desk was his watch. Ben and I had clubbed together one Christmas to buy it. It had been a whack but something Evan had been drooling over for months. And it had been on his wrist when I found him in my hallway. Subconsciously I rubbed at the scab on my arm where I had nicked my skin when I had pulled Evan's body into my lap.

Closing my eyes, I blew out a breath.

"Hello, Harley. Took you a while, princess."

The sound of Mole's voice behind me didn't make me jump. My heart didn't gallop. My body didn't lock down in panic.

I was angrier that I hadn't seen it, seen him. Once again my stupidity had outdone me.

"I was giving you a head start, Mole."

I needed to move but my legs wobbled, my feet unsure if they would hold me up if I did.

He laughed, the sick sound making the few items of Chow Mein I had eaten force their way up my dry throat. Swallowing, I finally turned. His smile morphed into a grin where he sat on a small chair under the staircase.

"Always in the dark, Jamie?"

His real name from me made him narrow his eyes, and he tutted. "You know better than that, Queenie."

I stood firm when he lifted his large body out of the chair, the wood creaking in appreciation after such a weight removed itself. His t-shirt clung to him, huge patches of sweat making the material almost see-through.

Yet, for such a fat guy, he could move. My throat was crushed under his fist in moments. "Now see, I'm a little concerned that some dumb bitch has been tittle-tattling."

"That would be me." I had no idea why I said that. I had no idea why I chose to wind the prick up, but hey, that's the way I, very stupidly, did things.

He quirked an eyebrow at my tone and tightened his grip. "It was all such a long time ago; you should have left it where it was. But you had to dig. You had to push. Michael is not very pleased."

"Fuck Michael!" I hissed, the sound of his name making my anger flare. I had got myself into this mess and it would be up to me to figure a way out. Although I wasn't doing such a great job right then. "He should be here, not you."

He laughed and my feet skidded when he started to push me backwards, the one hand around my throat holding me up. He was strong, as well as obese, I'd give him that. His eyes glinted when he pressed the edge of a blade between my breasts, slicing a nick into my t-shirt. "You really think that you were in control? You're even more stupid than he says you are."

"Oh, I'm stupid, alright. Just a dumb bitch me."

"I'll admit you're right there. You see, all your suffering was for nothing. I didn't make Michael suffer by fucking you; I never intended to. You were just part of the plan. He played you, you fell to his whim and just like that-" He clicked his fingers in my face. "My *partner* and I ruined Frank Davids' daughter. We could no longer ruin the man himself, so his offspring became the sacrifice."

"Don't mention my dad's name."

I spat in his face, gasping when he tightened his hold. The blood began rushing to my face, my cheeks swelling, eyes popping under the force.

"Frank fucking Davids. How's that Harley Queen?" I would have cried, but Mole held my bodily functions hostage. "What do you think good ol' Frankie would have done if he saw his precious daughter's cunt fucked raw? What would he have done if he walked in on your gaping arsehole, puke-covered sheets and your tear-stained porcelain face?"

I needed to cry. I needed to scream. I needed to do something, but I was captured, not only by Fat Jamie, but by the grief that slammed into me with the realisation that I'd missed it all.

"What did Frank have to do with it?" he asked as my mouth moved continuously, trying to form the first '*w*' of the question. "Well, maybe something. Maybe nothing. But knowledge will cost you, princess."

The blood drained from his face when my knee found his dick, his jaw dropping with the force as I rammed it into his groin. The second his hand loosened, I dipped under his arm and raced across the room. I just needed to reach my desk drawer. That was all I needed to do. I knew what he intended to do. He'd made me pay before and I had no intention of settling another debt that wasn't mine to suffer for. I ran as fast as I could, cursing my shaking legs and tight lungs.

Stars burst across my vision when my forehead smacked the edge of the desk and I was hoisted back by my ankles. My nose thudded on the tiles and the sudden pain made my brain squeal.

"That wasn't so wise," Mole growled as he pulled me harder. "Now you'll have to make the pain go away."

My eyes shot wide and I shook my head. "What? No, you can't...not again!"

His laugh made my blood freeze and I kicked out at him, but he caught my feet together, grasping them in just one of his giant hands as he grappled with the button of my jeans.

"No!" I screamed as he tore at his own trousers, pulling himself out and battling with me at the same time. He had a strength I was struggling to fight with, his total domination of a situation I thought I had been ready to control was my undoing.

I scratched at him, bit him, hit out at him but he laughed, and he took it like it turned him on, which in hindsight I knew it did. Would he have been so determined if I'd laid meekly and opened my legs for him? I couldn't answer that, because I would never know.

In one single movement, he flipped me over so I was face down. My heart stopped and my eyes closed as I forced myself to see Evan, to see the image of his handsome face, to hear the echo of his laughter in my head, and to feel his hand slip into mine as Mole kicked my legs open and crushed my face to the floor with a hand to the back of my head. The knife he'd ripped my shirt with dug into my ribs as he shredded my blouse and it fell away, leaving me cold and exposed.

"Time to play again, Harley Davids," Mole whispered in my ear as the head of his cock rubbed between my legs.

All I heard was my own whimper. All I felt was a complete numbness that trickled into my veins. All I saw was Evan's face. And all I wanted was to die.

But….it never came. Death, or rape. Neither found me. But insanity did.

Mole's weight suddenly vanished.
I rolled over, gasping for breath as I sought him out. I found him.
And then I found *him*…. No. I found *them*. Two of *him*. Two Carters staring down at me. The man I had found myself falling in love with was not one person, but two. Two men. Identical. Both with one blue eye and one green, both of them staring at me warily. Waiting for me to figure it out.
Stupidity. Stupid. I've been so damn stupid.
I couldn't look at him—them. It was too implausible. Improbable.

My heart stampeded. The roar of blood pounded in my ears. Tears fell from my eyes as I stared in horror, the sharp sting after not blinking for so long making my vision blur at the edges. The tightness in my chest grew and my lungs started to constrict as the bile stuck in my throat obstructed the oxygen needed to fill them.

I couldn't look away from the grotesque form laid out before me like a gift - which in a way I suppose he was, his very last breath an offering to me.

His dead eyes fixed on my horror-stricken ones, the blank stare mirroring mine. His head was bent at an angle that couldn't, *shouldn't*, be possible, the severe twist in his neck making his chin rest perfectly between his shoulder blades.

My head shook so hard the impact made my body tremble, my muscles constricting to stabilise the rattle in my bones. My jaw clenched when my teeth started to chatter. I was cold; so cold, the icy panic and reality of what lay before me seeping into the marrow of my bones and making me numb. The bass of the music beat in time with my heart, the sharp notes of whatever the singer was saying piercing my soul with every screech and squeal, every sensual hum that filled the void in her song. But not in me. I felt hollow, I felt empty; I felt like a part of me had evaporated when he died. When he was murdered. His life stolen from him before my eyes.

"Harley."

I blinked once, twice, as he called me again. His voice, low and seductive, firm and unforgiving, sent goose bumps to flare over my skin and burn against the coldness I felt. Finally, my stare shifted to find the source of the soft, coaxing voice. Eyes void of remorse bore into me, stealing the breath I was desperately trying to draw. He held me captive in his gaze, keeping me frozen to the spot, until he took a step towards me. On instinct, I shuffled back.

"No." I wasn't sure if I had even managed to speak the word or if my mind had just ordered it because I knew I should want him to stay away.

Nothing was real. Nothing made sense. But then, in so many ways, it did. While my eyes were struggling to define, my mind was sighing in relief. Every single one of my unanswered questions were finally satisfied. So many things that had made me doubt myself slotted into place, yet, still none of them made any sense. The conflict between my eyes and my brain was making me nauseous, and my stomach roiled as I fought to keep a retch contained.

"Let me..."

My head shook harder and I lifted my hands from where they rested on my stomach, attempting to stop him getting any closer. Of course he didn't obey my silent command...had I expected him to? *Did I want him to?* In my desperation to figure this out, rationalise what was happening, and force my mind to catch up to grant me some mercy, I needed to look away. I needed to not see, like I had been doing for so long. I needed the ignorance that once felt like a niggling ache for the truth; now it felt like I was being trampled by my own stupidity. They say ignorance is bliss...I could attest to that. I should have run while I had the chance.

My eyes ventured from him to my hands. Blood. So much blood. It coated my skin, dripping down my wrists and onto the floor. Flesh was buried deep under my fingernails, and a solitary pubic hair protruded from the edge of my thumbnail.

The bile that had been stuck in my throat spewed with the contents of my stomach and my knees buckled with the force of it, forcing me to crumble in on myself. My hands slapped onto the floor as another wave of vomit burst from me. My stomach churned and water dripped from my eyes as my sanity broke and I screamed with every single heave of devastation.

Shoes came into my line of sight and I scuttled back, huddling myself into the wall as I tried to back away from him. I was trapped between his menacing form and the wall that felt like cotton against his frightening glare. I knew he wouldn't hurt me, he would have done it already, right? But it didn't stop the panic now I'd seen what he *could* do...and it didn't stop me glancing behind him, around him, above him. Anything to make sense of what was happening.

"You're hurt," he said gently, lifting his own hands quickly to placate me as he dropped to crouch before me. "Let me help you."

Me.

But which one? Who was going to help me? Who was going to come to my rescue and, could I let them?

A wave of pain made my breath catch and my hands instinctively made to grab my belly. It was then I realised the blood that covered my hands was mine. Trickling. Pumping out with every beat of my heart. Soaking into my clothes as the adrenaline kicked in and told me to run. *Where have you been, adrenaline? I could have used this warning months ago.* The gash continued to seep and I became consciously aware of the pang of copper, the metallic smell so potent I could taste it. The pain. God, the pain. What had happened to me? How had I got here?

Out of it all...the dead man hideously still staring at me. The cruel break in my sanity. The vicious tremor racking my bones. The deafening rush of blood in my ears. The rapidly dimming double vision. The music that continued to pound, over and over, like a ticking time bomb. It had been counting down for some time - I realised that now. The few remaining grains of sand tumbled into the funnel to settle on a discarded pile of morality and with them, my mind began to slip. It was the sight of my own blood that forced my brain to offer me a reprieve and swallow me in the depths of unconsciousness.

Blackness consumed me as strong arms pulled me in.

Twenty-Six
H̸ARLEY

I woke up to the scent of betrayal. I wasn't in my home, in my bed. I was in his—*their*—home, in *their* bed. My eyes were heavy and the constant beeping of machines made me growl. I didn't open my eyes, but I could flex my fingers, and I did, over and over again.

"Harley…"

Whose voice was it? Carter 1 or Carter 2? I couldn't tell. Why the fuck couldn't I tell? How had I fallen for a man who was two men? They'd been playing me all along and I'd been the perfect fucking mouse to two savage, unfeeling cats.

"Harley," he said again.

"What?" I snapped. "What do you want?"

"How are you feeling?"

"Like you give a shit."

"At least she still has fire," the other Carter said.

The only way I could tell who was talking was to listen…go figure. I should have done that before. The first Carter was close to me, the other a few feet behind him. They were here, together, and I was stuck blind and immobile.

"Why am I here?" I asked, turning my head to gage my surroundings.

"Something happened," Carter 2 said.

"No shit, Sherlock."

"You were stabbed. I didn't see the knife when we came in. Jamie had it between you while he..." He paused and cleared his throat. "The knife went in as I killed him."

I didn't say anything. I remembered the blood. I remembered the pain. I felt the pain now, like it was happening all over again.

"You're here so I can look after you," he said.

I heard his smile, his beautiful fucking smile. I imagined his eyes sparkling as he looked at me, trying to hide that we were doing more than just fucking, because he cared. He really cared. Did he?

"What happened?"

My voice was croaky, my throat dry. I felt like I was trembling from the inside out, beginning in my spine and rippling out to make my fingers numb.

"Mole."

I screamed, my back arching off the bed as I gripped the sheets and cried out for the man who had ruined me—again.

"Don't say his name!"

"Open your eyes, babe."

"No. Don't say his fucking name again."

Visions of him lying on the floor in my basement, his gut exposed by his lack of pants and the shirt that had slipped up his body with the force of him being dragged away from me. I remembered the way he looked at me, like a filthy cannibal ready to eat me alive just because I was Frank Davids' daughter. Why? What did my dad have to do with the mess that had become my life since the day he'd been killed?

"You ruined everything," I said, falling back into an almost sedate state.

"He was going to kill you."

"I know."

Silence descended over the room as the reality of what I'd said sunk in. I'd been prepared to die. I hadn't killed Michael and I'd given up, in my basement, with Jamie on top of me promising to eat me alive, make me bleed out like Evan, my parents, and Henry, my beautiful baby brother. I'd given up, resigned to dying because I didn't believe anyone had the ability to save me. Mole wasn't supposed to come for me, but he had…and it turned out he'd held all the answers I would now never have.

"What did we ruin, babe?" Carter 1 asked, taking hold of my hand.

I tried to pull away, but he was too strong. He linked his fingers with mine and settled them both on my stomach. I hated that I loved it. I hated that I loved it just as much when another hand took mine and held it on the bed.

"No," I said, shaking my head and forcing my muscles to relax so I couldn't hold either of them back. "I'm done being the toy. If you want me to let you in, you have to make the first move. I'm done being in the dark."

"My name is Rome Carter," Carter 1 said, stroking his thumb over the back of my hand.

I recognised him as the man who was the neat-freak. The way he stroked my hand to illicit comfort he was convinced he lacked the ability to do, made me acutely aware of all the times he'd been with me. He'd met me on my run, he'd taken me for coffee... the one who had found me with Bill in the gallery and held me with a little more force than necessary.

"And I'm Jobe Carter," Carter 2 said, immediately drawing my attention to the spark in his voice.

He was a live-wire. He was the Carter I'd met in the club, the one who had held me against the window in the apartment.... he'd been with me when I found Evan.

I noticed it now, the subtle differences in them. Why hadn't I noticed them before and seen beyond the lies?

"I would say it's nice to meet you," I seethed, taking a deep breath as my chest began to tighten. "But really, I'm just looking forward to never having to see you again."

"Rome and Jobe operate as one person," Rome continued. "For many reasons, pretty girl. Mainly because one man can't be a hitman and run the city's most successful nightclub at the same time, and an alibi is always constant, of course. There are a handful of people in the world who know there are two of us, and you've now made that very short list."

"So you see," Jobe continued, his edgy deviance creeping over me. He was—or at least appeared to be—the most unstable. "We can't just let you leave."

"I'm not going to tell. You know I've got nothing left and you ruined all hope I had of finding a future."

"Babe," one of them said. I couldn't tell which. The way they said 'babe', radiated with the same hunger and conflicting adoration, was the same, regardless of which tongue it rolled from. "We're helping you. The mission isn't over. Whatever this is between us…it's far from over."

"It's a sick love triangle I have no interest in. I've been shared around enough." I sat up, keeping my eyes squeezed shut despite the urge to look and see my nightmare in the flesh. "You knew that and you exploited it."

"Dude, just leave her. She's difficult as fuck and we've got to track Michael down."

Rome had said that, but it was something that I had suddenly attributed to the Jobe Carter I'd spent time with. He spoke like his brother, but in the confusing way that snagged my attention and ensnared me like a moth to a flame. I was drawn to both of them, equally, inexplicably, and hopelessly.

I was done.

"Yeah, you should go."

Sliding back down the bed, I winced when the sharp twinge in my stomach stole my breath and I curled up in the foetal position.

"Hey," Jobe said, reaching out to stroke my hair away from my face. "We'll look after you. I told you that you can trust me. You can trust us both. You've cracked the code, and everything will be alright."

What the fuck was he on? I pulled my body away from him, forcing myself to breathe through the pain, until I'd heard them both leave and close the door behind them.

Then, and only then, did I allow a tear to fall.

After the first incident, Rome and Jobe visited me separately, bringing me food and drinks, walking me to the bathroom, and standing outside while I showered.

I morphed into a shell of my former self, and when I began to feel the effects of cocaine withdrawal, I realised why they were keeping me here. I was given an iPad and I used it to google the effects of going cold turkey on Cloud. First on the list was a crash, and I'd suffered a write-off. I realised that every ounce of confidence I'd possessed, every slice of aggression that had kept me focussed, was because of cocaine. Without it I was nothing but a vessel harbouring shame and regret. Second on the list was intense craving. I'd stooped lower than I ever would have imagined going, screaming from my bed for Carter—either one—to give me a hit. Just one hit. I needed it. I *needed* it. They hadn't given in, refusing to budge. Instead of giving in to my demands and the negotiations I'd tried to make, they locked me in the bedroom, turned the music up, and had a party in the penthouse apartment of Chimera. I fucking hated them for it...until symptom number four arrived—fatigue. I was so tired. I slept most of every day away, waiting for the cravings and willingness to shamelessly offer things in exchange for the only thing I had left to fade. It took weeks. Sickness ravaged my body, making me puke throughout the day, until my cravings for Cloud morphed into hunger for endless bowls of Coco-Pops and ice cold milk. I was irritable and aggressive, striking Carter—either one—every time they came too close, or spoke in a way that made it impossible to know who I was talking to. They took it, allowing me to battle with my own mind, and I saw the hope in their bicoloured eyes that I would make it through the tunnel. Paranoia stole me from fully functioning as a human. Why were they keeping me here? What did they want? What would happen if I pushed too far? Was this the end? Were they just delaying the inevitable before they rammed a bullet in my skull?

"Harley!"

Rome shot into the room when I'd finished my bowl of Coco-Pops and tried hacking at my wrists with my spoon. He stole it from my grasp and threw it across the room as Jobe burst in, attracted by the rough growl that left his brother. I flinched, bringing my knees up to my chest as far as I could, and shuffling backwards to press my back to the leather headboard.

"For fuck's sake, Harley."

"Don't." I snapped, smacking him away and pulling the duvet up to my neck. "Don't judge me when I'm stuck in here, reduced to a prisoner. A fucking junkie worth nothing!"

"That's not what we think, pretty girl," Jobe said, joining his brother on the bed on the other side of me. "We need you to break this addiction. When you have, you can come out and we'll work through this."

Now he was talking like Rome, the soft side they both hated to expose breaking free. I gripped two fistfuls of hair and stared between them.

"I can't do this."

"Babe…"

"It's not the addiction. I'm over it," I lied, knowing the only way to get through to them. "I can't stand…"

"Go on," Jobe said, excitement lighting up his eyes. The green one became a meadow warmed by the summer sun, and the blue one became the Caribbean ocean, vibrant and breath-taking.

"I…"

"Is it the frustration?" Rome asked, drawing my attention from his brother to him.

He licked his full bottom lip and snagged it between his teeth. I nodded.

"It's common," Jobe said, snaring my gaze again. "It's okay."

"It's not okay," I clipped, each word accentuated and aggressive.

"It's just a side-effect," Rome said, placing his hand on my knee and encouraging me to straighten my legs. He settled his hand on my thigh when I'd complied.

Shaking my head, I whispered, "It's not."

"So what is it?"

"Confusion."

It wasn't a lie. I was confused. I was conflicted. I needed to bring the two halves of my soul, half in Jobe's grasp and the other half belonging to Rome, back together.

"Have you tried?" Jobe asked, tucking a strand of hair behind my ear before his hand mirrored Rome's. "To make yourself come?"

I nodded. I had. I'd been alone for weeks, after months of sex with not just one virile man with stamina to match the gods, but with two of them—replicas. Twins. I'd tried every night for the past week, to part my legs and close my eyes as I imagined Carter—when he was just one man—making me come like only he could. It hadn't worked, not once. I couldn't find an ounce of pleasure by my own hand, and I knew it wasn't because cocaine withdrawal led to the inability to feel pleasure.

"Have you thought about doubling the stimulant?" Rome asked, squeezing my thigh. I jumped and, for the first time in weeks, heat flared deep in my core and I closed my legs.

"W-what?"

"Well, Harley..." Jobe's thumb dug into the soft flesh and I stilled, focussing on the tiny shred of stimulation as he circled the digit and looked at Rome. "One man might not be enough to pop the cork on your inability to come, but what about..."

"Two men," Rome whispered, leaning over me to kiss my neck. I sighed, but shook my head.

"I'm not that girl," I lied. A blatant fucking lie. "I'm not going to give you reason to punish me for fucking you both."

"Clever girl," Rome said as his teeth grazed the sensitive spot behind my ear. "But we're not going to punish you. What happens when you fall for twins?"

"I didn't know you were a twin!"

I tried to push him away, but he chuckled, sending goose bumps over my skin. A second pair of lips touched my neck as Jobe mirrored his brother's actions.

"What happens when twins fall for the same girl?" Jobe asked. "Are we supposed to fight over who has you?" I shook my head. "And then we figured, why can't we both have you?"

"I'm scared you're playing me. This isn't right."

"This started as a game, babe," Rome said, grabbing my breast and squeezing hard.

"It has become an obsession," Jobe added, scraping his nails over my nipple, hard and erect under my t-shirt.

"I..."

"Shh..." they whispered together, each of them taking one of my legs and parting them, pinning me beneath their bodies.

"I just..."

"Want to come?"

I nodded.

"Want to figure this strange connection out?"

I nodded again.

"So do we."

The duvet was whipped off me, and it settled somewhere on the floor across the room. Rome tore at my t-shirt, sucking a nipple into his mouth while he massaged the other breast in his rough hand. Jobe gripped my underwear and tore it in two, cupping my pussy and sinking a finger in deep. I threw my head back and moaned. I didn't care how loud. I didn't care how needy. I was safe with the Carters and they'd given me permission to let my whore free in their bed. Jobe's fingers fucked me with abandon, his mouth closing around my other nipple as Rome reached between us and dexterous fingers found my clit. I bucked against them, wrapping my arms around their shoulders to watch them take control of my body. The groans and moans of approval that left through their parted lips made me arch my back in a silent plea for more.

Grabbing my wrist, Rome guided my hand between us and settled my palm over the hard bulge in his pants. Without instruction, my free hand moved between Jobe's legs and I stroked them simultaneously. Our breaths became a heavy cocktail of lust and forbidden desire. Our moans became a symphony of deviance. Our hands roamed harder, hips ground with fervour and, eventually, my mouth was seized by Rome, his tongue forcing its way inside my mouth to show me just how much this *was not* a game. He tasted of beer and cigarettes. I was fascinated by him, meeting his tongue with my own so I could explore this and figure it out, like they'd said.

Wait…did they expect *me* to choose?

I broke free from Rome's mouth and gasped, my lips swollen and tingling from his assault. Before I could cry and ask them if this was their game plan, Jobe crashed his lips to mine, filling my mouth with the flavour of the same beer as his brother, and the subtle taste of weed. I gripped the back of his neck as Rome's lips skated down my body. His teeth grazed my stomach and over my hip bones as his brother took my bottom lip between his teeth and resumed the kiss. My back arched when Rome dived between my legs and his mouth covered my pussy as he sucked hard on my clit.

"God!" I cried, pushing Jobe away to take a breath.

He didn't let me take a break; he straddled me, freeing his cock from his pants and stroking his erection just inches from my face. I licked my lips, desperate to touch him, but my arms were trapped beneath his body.

"Do you want it, Harley?" he asked, running his thumb over my bottom lip before the head of his cock followed. My tongue sneaked out to taste him—just a taste. "Do you think you can tell the difference in the taste? In the way we'll swell inside your mouth and jerk against your tongue?"

I nodded. I was confident. I'd never been more confident in my life. Carter—both of them—were mine and I wouldn't allow my mind to shield me from the truth again. I had fallen in love with twins. Rome's tongue dived inside me as his fingers pinched my clit, and as I threw my head back to cry out, Jobe halted my breath with his thick smooth cock sliding between my lips. I choked, my eyes opening wide as he held the back of my head and thrust in and out slowly, allowing me to map out every vein and ridge along his delicious length. My body tightened, trembling under the mouth of Rome, the pressure from Jobe filling my mouth, and the reality that these boys owned me.

"That's it, babe," Jobe said, stroking my cheek as Rome groaned against my sensitive flesh. "Come for us."

I would. I knew I would. It was overdue. I'd been pent up and frustrated for weeks as I battled my addiction and the chemical imbalance in my brain that told me I was fucking mental for doing this. But it was Carter—both of them—who were making me come now, rewriting everything I thought made me *me*. Would I go back, and undo the new coding they'd programmed into my soul?

Not a fucking chance.

"Oh, God," I cried as my body built to a crescendo that had me writhing beneath my lovers and begging for something. Anything.

Rome growled against me, tipping me over the edge as Jobe stilled inside me and allowed me to feel him pulse against my tongue. The single drip of pre-cum that trickled down my throat was my undoing and I shattered, plummeting to Earth with a soul-shattering scream. Jobe pulled out and as I trembled and shuddered, I was vaguely aware of them switching places. My eyes widened when, for the first time, I noticed the difference between the two brothers. Rome's bare chest was covered with marks – cigarette burns and welts that married with my own. Jobe, having straddled me not moments ago, had a smooth and unmarked chest.

My mouth was filled again, breaking me from my discovery, but my arms were free and I reached behind Rome to grip his ass. My ankles were raised off the bed and my legs wrapped around a lean body as Jobe nudged against me, flexing oh so gently until he slid past my barriers and sunk balls deep inside me.

"Ah!" I cried, a garbled moan of pleasure against Rome's cock. He stilled and slipped both hands in my hair.

"Christ, Harley," he murmured, squeezing until I felt the pressure on my skull, initiating a feeling of delirium no amount of Cloud could rival. "You suck cock like a pro."

Spurred on by his compliment, I took hold of him, fisting him in one hand while I gripped his balls in the other. I shunted up the bed as Jobe picked up the pace, slamming into me until my eyes watered and my stomach tightened in preparation to explode.

I knew I should have felt degraded, and I did.

I knew I should have felt used, and I did.

I knew I should have felt out of control, dominated, and I did.

But I fucking loved it.

I was soon moaning with abandon, gasping around Rome's cock as his salty pre-cum dripped onto my tongue and down my throat, and the wetness between my legs provided Jobe with everything he needed to take my body to impossible heights. I cried as the hint of another orgasm teased my core with every synchronised thrust from *my* twins, every animalistic grunt that left them providing a soundtrack for our unconventional grouping. It was relief. It was a tsunami of emotions after feeling nothing but numbness and hunger for weeks. It was a technical repair after years of being lost, floating along and waiting for someone to program me back to life.

The Carter twins had done that and I loved them for it.

I came with a scream, working Rome's cock as I threw my head back and gasped for breath. I watched his stomach tighten and felt his thighs tense around me, as Jobe's thrusts became uneven, rough, and frantic.

"That's it, babe," Rome said through gritted teeth. "Make me come."

I would. God, I would. I squeezed my legs around Jobe, urging him to come for me while I made his brother explode. My arm ached and my wrist felt tight, but I didn't stop, desperate to see him lost in bliss. He came with a loud cry, throwing his head back as his chest reddened, the vein in his neck pumped furiously, and he exploded into my waiting mouth. His cum jetted onto my tongue, over my lips and onto my chin, and I swallowed, licking my lips to catch every drop. He collapsed over me, resting his hands either side of my head as he eased back into my mouth, jerking with sensitivity. Jobe gripped my hips, falling forward to press his forehead between his brother's shoulder blades as he grunted and I felt the first hot spurt of his cum fill me.

"Fuck," he groaned, pulling out of me and laying on his back beside me.

"Fuck," Rome breathed, falling to the other side of the me, on his stomach.

I looked at Jobe as sweat trickled from his temple, soaked his chest, and lined his top lip. I leaned forward and kissed him, catching the salty perspiration. I glanced at Rome as he drew delicate patterns on my stomach, keeping my attention on him and not the scars on my body that made me hideous. His hair was a sweat-matted mess, perspiration lining his eyebrows and I leaned closer to kiss him and taste it. I laid back, staring first at Jobe, and then at Rome, as both men looked at me for my reaction. I only had one thing to say.

"Fuck."

Twenty-Seven
ROME

Mum was passed out again. I'd helped her, but only because I wanted to play video games and hide in the bedroom. She didn't like me playing video games. When she was awake she needed attention. She needed a grown-up with her, and grown-ups—at least my mum's friends—were dangerous. She'd asked for my belt and I'd taken it off and given it to her. She'd asked me to pull tight and I had, shoving my foot against the sofa so I could pull as tight as I could. She'd asked me to pass her the syringe, and I'd thought about handing her two. But then, when she woke up, she'd need to get another and...my bruises hadn't healed from the last time she paid with my face. She hadn't let me inject her, but she'd made me watch while she did it. I was supposed to be on guard, make sure she didn't have a seizure or start vomiting everywhere. I wasn't allowed to let her choke. She didn't want to die—dead people couldn't get high. I'd watched until her eyes rolled and she slumped back on the sofa...and then I went upstairs to leave her to her high.

"Hey," I said, stepping in the room and sitting next to Jobe.

He had Mario set up and handed me the controller. We sat on the floor and took it in turns to complete a level. I'd given Jobe the watch I got for

Christmas and he kept checking it, knowing we didn't have long before she woke up. I managed to get us some crisps from the kitchen and glasses of water from the tap. It was a bit brown, definitely not healthy; a pipe had burst last week and Mum was too high to call the landlord and ask him to get it fixed. Tony, the landlord, doubled up as one of our mum's dealers. He supplied her with the crack. Andrew sold her the meth. Ralph kept her topped up with heroine. It was only a matter of time before she died, and both Jobe and I were waiting for it. We didn't know what we'd do or where we go, but at least we wouldn't have to be the tourniquet fixers or spoon-gatherers anymore.

"Boys?"

We jumped when a booming voice wafted through the house. Jobe looked at me. I looked at him. Mario fell and we lost our last life. Damn it, that wasn't a good sign.

I recognised the voice and knew what would come next. Verbal abuse for one twin. More bruises for the other. Andrew's heavy footsteps pounded up the stairs and we stared at the door. It smashed open, banging against the wall behind as Andrew filled the space with his arms folded, feet apart.

"Yes?" I asked, getting to my knees and sitting in front of Jobe.

He'd had it harder than I had. Sticks and stones may break your bones, but mental abuse ruined your soul.

"Mamma still high?" he asked. I nodded. "Oh good. I thought I'd take an advance payment while she's out of it."

I rolled my eyes and turned my head to see Jobe in my peripheral, frozen in fear and wondering what he'd hear this time.

"Go for it," I said, deciding that if I was the little shit, he'd leave Jobe be.

"Shall we have a little chat?"

I shook my head. Chats meant his fists weren't participating, which meant I was safe and my brother was in danger of another battering that would ruin him a little bit more. Andrew crossed the room and laid on my bed, shoving one hand behind his head as the other grabbed my tennis ball off the cabinet and he tossed it up in the air.

"Do you know why your mother named you what she did?" he asked.

I shook my head and turned to face him, noticing Jobe had blanched. He knew today's story would have a bad ending for him.

"Let me tell you," he said, glancing between us with a stupid smirk. I wanted to kill him, but I knew that wouldn't help either of us. "Rome, your mother named you Rome because you're strong and powerful. While your brother was failing in the womb, you thrived. Jobe, you were a pathetic little shit, even as an embryo."

"Nothing to do with our mother's habit, I suppose?" I said, quirking an eyebrow. "So I assume she can't take the blame for risking her child's life."

Andrew shrugged. He didn't really care about that part of the story. He had the tale planned and there was no room for deviation, for development beneath the narrative. Yeah, I listened in English class. I wanted to be clever so I could avoid turning out like our mother and her prick-head dealers.

"Jobe, your name is Hebrew for 'persecuted'. Do you know what persecuted means, little shit?"

Jobe nodded. He'd been told his entire life why he was the neglected child, while I took all the golden showers in some sick representation of why I was the fucking favourite. Because of my name. Stupid, huh? My name was also the capital of Italy—where the mafia ruled the fucking country. I chose to follow that path; I'd kill all the fuckers who punished my brother because of his fucking name.

"It means abused, harassed...victimised. Do you feel victimised, boy?" When Jobe nodded, Andrew laughed, throwing his head back into my pillow and gripping his stomach in over-exaggeration. "No, no. You were named Jobe because you annoyed the shit out of your mother. She only wanted one child—a junkie with a kid gets all the sympathy her rotting little heart desires. When Rome came out, healthy and plump, she had what she needed. Then you, you little weed...you popped out next, but she already had her ticket to druggie-heaven. She didn't need you and you became an annoyance, a punishment...you became her persecution so she named you appropriately."

"You're such a cunt," I spat, throwing my shoe at his head.

Once upon a time, Jobe cried when he was faced with abuse. Now, he felt nothing. He felt worthless. He felt like an annoyance. My mother and all her stupid fuckheads had won. They'd beaten him and I'd made it my mission to repair him piece by beautiful piece. My brother was the clever one, the perceptive one, the one who took the abuse and decided he was to blame.

Me? I'd decided I'd grow up to be a hitman and murder every fucking prick who made someone suffer like my brother did.

"What did you say?" Andrew said, sitting up and rubbing the red spot on his head, imprinted with the sole of my shoe.

"I said you're a cunt."

Andrew seethed, almost foaming at the mouth like a rabies-infested dog. It was the kind of reaction I was supposed to look for when she got high.

"That's a mighty word for a little prick," he spat.

I shrugged one of my shoulders. "Not my fault it's the truth."

I knew what I was doing. He'd told his story; he knew he'd broken Jobe a little more inside. Our mother's hope was that he would top himself, see his life as nothing worth living. It was my job to keep him alive, to fill him with hope for a future—for both of us. Andrew lunged at me, like I'd hoped he would, grabbing me by the throat, yanking me to my feet and slamming me against the wall. The first punch made my eye swell shut, but I saw Jobe out of my good eye. I heard him crying, wanting to beg Andrew to let me go, but we'd had a deal. I'd made him promise to let me take it, and patch me up afterwards.

"It amazes me that your mother hasn't traded you both in to all the nonses for a fix."

"She knows sick fucks like you get off on abusing kids. Way more rewarding."

The next punch hit the side of my head, and my vision blurred. The third punch split my lip. The fourth sent my back teeth through my cheek. I laughed through the pain, through the agony swimming in my veins, and spat my blood at Andrew. The fifth and final punch brought the blackness to smother me.

"Rome?"

I woke up in my bed, the smell of Andrew's cigarettes surrounding me as music played downstairs and I knew our mother was awake— entertaining.

"I'm here," I answered, opening my eye as Jobe shook me awake. "All good."

I was not all good. I hurt like a bitch. I knew I'd taken kicks to the ribs, a stamp to the back and...my chest stung. God, it felt like fire.

"He burned you," Jobe said, a single tear falling from his eye.

"Ahh..." I smiled, like I'd figured it out, but Jesus, I felt like I had no skin left on my chest. I. Was. In. Agony. But I reminded myself, as I assessed my brother and sighed in relief when I noticed he was pain free—physically, at least. He was okay. I'd won another day. "I'm alright."

"I counted," he said, gripping my elbow to help me sit up. "Fifteen burns. He went through fifteen cigarettes one after the other while you were passed out."

"Did he touch you?" Jobe shook his head and looked down at his knotted fingers. "Then we win."

"I was thinking..."

He stopped, doubting himself. Convinced his idea was bullshit before he'd even shared it.

"Go on."

"What if we stopped being twins."

"We've talked about this," I snapped. "You go, I go."

"That's what I mean. What if we both go?"

"Like a fucking suicide pact?" I sat up quickly, searching for a weapon he'd collected, or drugs he'd stolen from our mother. "Dude, we've got shit to do when we grow up."

"I know." He laughed. It was the crazy laugh I'd begun to notice in him. He was a little bit insane—a product of being made to feel worthless. "I mean...what if Jobe and Rome were no longer two people."

"What are you saying?"

"I think we should become one. We can't let anyone play us off against each other again..."

"You ever think we'd be here?" Jobe asked, pulling me from the past as he leaned back on the sofa and took an almighty pull on his joint. He laughed. "I mean, after Mum and Charlotte."

I laughed, taking the spliff from him and snagging a drag. "Did I ever think our combined identities would come back to bite us?" I shook my head. "Nah."

"We're not going to hurt her, are we?"

I shook my head again. "We can't. We don't shy away from responsibility. We did this, we have to fix it."

Jobe nodded, retrieving his joint and nodding at me to refill our glasses with whisky. I complied. We'd fucked up, of course we had. We were never supposed to fall in love again—not after Charlotte played us off against each other and broke our hearts. We had then, you see. We weren't unfeeling psychopaths; we just decided, at a young age, that the only way to protect ourselves was to hide behind each other, behind our surname, Carter. If we lived as one, played as one, existed as one, we couldn't be hurt again. But that was before Harley fucking Davids. She wasn't just a master hacker behind a computer. She'd hacked into our identity and separated it back into two. And then she'd made both of them fall in love with her. We were fucked, and yet, this was the most whole we'd felt in twenty years of combined existence.

"Any news on Michael?" I asked, throwing my arms to the back of the sofa.

"Nothing yet. The cunt has disappeared."

"She won't move on until he's dead. We're all stuck in limbo, dude."

"We'll find him," Jobe reassured. "We've called in every one of our favours. He'll slip up and when he does, we'll get him."

I nodded, marginally reassured. The bedroom door clicked open and both Jobe and I turned to look towards the bedroom. Harley emerged, dressed in my t-shirt and Jobe's boxers. She was as torn as the both of us. She wouldn't choose between the two of us because both of us had played with her, coerced her into being irrevocably tied to the two of us. Jobe and I never fought—we never would, so the only answer was to share Harley and hope she wouldn't turn on us and become another Charlotte. It was a risk, but we'd played it safe for years and it was time to lay it all on the table. She was too strong to let us break her, and we were too devoted to her to even try.

"Hey," she said, joining us on the sofa and glancing at the joint in Jobe's hand. He shook his head and leaned forward to stub it out. "I wasn't going to ask."

Good. Because we weren't going to let her. We'd let her in, told her who we really were, but there was still one vital, life-altering secret we were keeping from her.

"What was her name?" she asked. Jobe and I looked at each other, without a clue what she was talking about. "The girl who broke you."

"What makes you think there was a chick?" I asked.

"Come on." She laughed and reached for the whisky. I snatched it away from her. "I'm not stupid. The only reason to share women to such the extent you do is because a woman pushed you to it."

"Charlotte Johnson," Jobe said, earning a warning glare from me. He shrugged. No point in keeping more secrets than we had to. "Gareth Johnson's sister."

Harley gasped and gripped the edge of the sofa, but she didn't break. I couldn't believe I'd expected her to. She'd been so fucked up, had so much confusion thrown at her that nothing would break her now.

"You ruined everything," she said. She'd been saying the same thing for weeks, but never explained herself. "Bill Clancy was supposed to protect me from Michael. I went out with him willingly. I needed him to fall in love with me so he would hide me when Michael finally came for me." Jobe and I growled in unison. We'd killed the cunt, and had a very good reason to. Harley was ours. *Ours.* "And Mole knew something about my family's murder. You killed the only two people who had answers."

"Perhaps," Jobe said, nodding at me to continue.

"But you're forgetting you're in love with two people who will leave no stone unturned to help you."

"What do you mean?" she asked, pouting when she reached for the whisky again and I refused to let her have it. "Seriously?"

"Seriously," I chastised. "Your father was a...*technical* man."

"My father was a hacker. That's no secret to me."

"We know." Jobe nodded, shifting to get comfortable. "It's the risk you take when you infiltrate people's lives without a trace. There's always the risk you'll hack the wrong man, leave a trail, open yourself up and leave yourself vulnerable."

"Okay..."

"Your father hacked a man called James Forester. He was instructed to clean his bank account and forward it to a woman named Claire Rathbone."

"Why?"

"James knocked her up." I shuddered. "It was a trap. It was James himself who instructed him to do it, and placed a tracker on your father. James was a powerful man, none other than Jamie Forester, Mole's, father. The Foresters were notorious hackers, working with the government with unlimited resources. Your father was a rival and, unfortunately, that was enough to secure his hit."

"Please tell me you didn't."

Harley covered her mouth, her paranoia and knowledge of who we were making her suspicious.

"No, we didn't. We're just as fucking skilled as the Forester's, with as many fucking contacts and a much better reputation."

"So how did you find out?"

"The Foresters were under surveillance, which is why Jamie went underground after his father's death from the big C. It's why he became Mole. There's a file on him in the database. We found it and put two and two together. We're not sure of Michael's involvement..."

"But mark our words, Harley," Jobe said, reaching over to take her hand. "You'll have every fucking explanation you deserve before we kill him."

Harley cried. She rested her elbows on her knees, buried her face in her hands and sobbed. It was chemical. It was emotional. It was real—so fucking real. Both Jobe and I got up and pulled her into us. There was no competition for her to accept more of the embrace from one of us, and there was no favouritism from her—no attempt to lean further into one of us than the other. She took us both and she loved us both with the same fierceness we'd come to love her with.

"Thank you," she said, wiping her eyes on my shoulder before doing the same on Jobe's. Always equal. I loved her more for it. "Thank you."

We held her until our knees went numb and her tears had run dry. When she released us and sat back, she smiled sadly.

"I love you," she said, somehow looking into both of our eyes at the same time. "I love you both so much. All I can do is apologise for dragging you into this. I'm not Charlotte."

"I know." I stroked her hair.

"We're both crazy in love with you." Jobe stroked her cheek.

"We're going to figure this out," I said, as I squeezed her knee and jerked her to lay back on the sofa with her ass over the edge.

"There's never been a story like ours before," Jobe said, parting her legs as a coy smile decorated her stunning fucking face. We were fucked. All of us. "We get to decide how it ends."

Twenty-Eight
JOBE

"I've found him!"

I jerked awake from where I'd fallen asleep on the sofa. I glanced across at Rome who hadn't woken from Harley's frantic outcry. Getting up, I pulled on my tracksuit bottoms and kicked my brother. He jolted awake, rolling off the sofa and reaching for his shorts.

"She's found him."

I raced towards the office with Rome not far behind me, and stormed into the room to see Harley tapping away at the keyboard. She had all three screens open, black boxes with vivid green code scrolling faster than I could read it.

"He was pulled over for speeding on the M11." She pointed at the code, copying and swiping onto another screen to copy into a textbox and bring up the information. "Charged with drink driving. Posted bail sixteen hours ago."

"Can you trace it back?" Rome asked, rubbing sleep from his eyes.

He'd taken the night shift last night to watch over her and the poor fucker hadn't slept. Pair that with the stress of finding the cunt who abused our girl—*our* fucking girl—and the rampant sex we'd had with our personal nymph, and he was fucking exhausted.

Harley, wrapped in the blanket from the back of the sofa, glanced over her shoulder at us, flipping us a visual 'fuck you' for doubting her skills. Her hair was wild and unruly, matted over on her shoulder, stray strands falling across her face. Her eyes were filled with vengeful excitement. She was ready. After weeks of rehab, suffering, grieving and throwing up at all hours of the day, she was back to her fiery, sassy self, and I'd be lying if I said it didn't boil my blood with lust and the need to feel her excitement as she came all over my cock.

"Of course I can fucking track it." She grinned and turned back to the computer, her fingers tapping away at an impossible speed. "He's staying at a hotel just out of town. Dumb shit didn't think we'd be tracking Mole's cards. He paid with an Am-Ex and hasn't checked out yet."

"Get dressed," Rome growled.

"Dude." I placed my hand on his shoulder. "You should sleep first. There are...preparations to be made."

I hoped, nodding my head in his direction and lifting my eyebrows to remind him of our predicament—the anomaly that had joined us uninvited but not entirely unwelcome, would snap him out of the single track his mind had taken.

"No fucking time. We end this now." Leaning over, he plucked Harley from the chair and carried her in the direction of the bedroom.

He'd lost it. The obsession to protect Harley like he used to protect me when we were kids had sent him spiralling into blindness and I knew devastation would find us soon. Sighing, I decided I'd have to remain in control, and took Harley's place at the desk to make the necessary preparations. We were going to get Michael and it was down to me to make sure the three of us left the hotel intact.

Harley and Rome emerged from the bedroom dressed as I pulled on my clothes in the living room. They both looked ready but, much like when I was a kid, I was doubting this. We'd never been this personal, never allowed our emotions to get in the way of a job, because feelings got people killed. I was the worthless twin, you see. There was no point in feeling much because I would be persecuted for it. It was in my name. But I'd fallen in love with Harley, and everything that had been created as a result, and I would protect her with everything I had in my worthless soul.

"Let's go," I said, tossing Rome the keys and grabbing Harley's hand.

We couldn't fuck this up. The future of all of us was relying on us ending this. Today.

Twenty-nine
HARLEY

"Fuck!" Rome hissed, his fists clenched as he stood and looked around at the empty and spotlessly clean hotel room.

"We've been played," Jobe sighed as if he'd known. *We should have known.*

Michael wasn't stupid. Far from it. Yet it still didn't make sense. "But why bring us here?" I muttered, chewing my lip as I wrestled to make my brain work.

Both my men shook their heads, feeling my frustration. It had been all too easy, and I should have counted on Michael's intelligence, but it still didn't make any damn sense. Why here? Why lay a trail to bring us here?

I licked my lips, the need for a recreational stimulant making my skin crawl and I shivered. Jobe slipped his hand into mine and shook his head. "Think, babe. Think what would he do now?"

"Michael will be laughing at us." I mused, the memories of his sick and twisted humour churning the Coco-Pops I had devoured earlier in the day. "He'll be watching us, and knowing he's won will make him giddy. Make him want to score." I held my breath. "I need to find out who his dealer is."

Rome narrowed his eyes on me. "That's too risky for you at the moment. There's no way you're fucking traipsing around all the known dealers…"

I shook my head. "I can do that from my house. It isn't like the sixties anymore, Rome. There's electronic records that are veiled, camouflaged as regular goods sale documents, even drug dealers like to keep their records up to date."

He looked doubtful but shrugged. "Fine."

I rushed from the room, eagerness for the end making my mouth dry. "Chew!" Jobe barked at me as he slipped me a piece of gum "It's supposed to help."

I looked at the gum sceptically but gave him a smile and thanked him as I popped it into my mouth and concentrated on every chew. Both him and Rome flanked me, each of them cocooning me protectively. My heart flipped and swelled in my chest. I loved them both. It was really that simple. I wasn't sure how, or even where, life would go from here, but I had a feeling they had already decided it for me. Forwards. With both of them. I should have been horrified at that, except I wasn't. I was excited, warm with hope and love for the first time in a very long while. Our relationship was as unique as their eyes. What should have been one was two. They had given each other a piece of themselves before they were even born, split their irises and their souls. And now I was included in their extraordinary coding, creating something that had never been formulated before.

My veins trembled with excitement. Michael would need a lot of shit to ride his high, and if we could find his dealer then we'd find Michael. I smiled, for the first time in a long time, I fucking smiled. "I'm coming for you, you piece of shit," I muttered under my breath. "I'm coming."

As always, everything fired up as we all descended into the basement. Rome took my desk as I took Evan's. Jobe hovered behind us, cracking his fingers rather annoyingly as I started to modify a program Evan had written to hunt out unadulterated files hidden covertly under any fabricated ones. Even in death my best friend was assisting, and I couldn't hold back the grin when his unique coding fired up and started to scroll down my screen, my fingers already adapting it for what I needed.

"What do you need me to do?" Rome asked as he looked at me, his fingers hovered over the keyboard awaiting my instruction.

"Do you know what you're doing?"

He quirked an eyebrow and said nothing, his expression saying everything.

"Okay," I smirked. "Sorry. I need you to open my connection with the NS database..."

"You hacked into the national security database?" Jobe asked, his eyes wide with shock but his smile full of pride. "My girl is fucking awesome."

I beamed at him. "I have been trying to tell you this for a long time." I blew him a kiss before I turned back to Rome. "You need to input Michael's name alongside Mole's, and give it some keywords to work though. It should do what we need it to and compile a list of associated dealers for us."

Rome nodded and turned to face the screen. A shiver tracked its way up my spine, biting into every single vertebra before it exploded in my brain, and time seemed to slow down when Evan's voice whispered in my ear. "Noooo."

But it was too late.

I'd been too eager to even notice it. Too fucking stupid to see it.

"Noooo!" I screamed.

But it was too late.

As soon as Rome's finger pressed the 'enter key' Michael's virus hit my kit.

"DO NOT TAKE YOUR FINGER OFF ENTER!" I screamed at Rome, diving across the room and slamming my hand down on his to stop him from moving.

His face blanched, his whole body freezing as his eyes widened on the screen in front of him.

"Harley?" Jobe whispered.

I couldn't move. I couldn't breathe. My heart didn't beat.

"Hello, my Harley Queen," Michael's face grinned back at us from the screen. "Figured it out, baby? Well," he laughed. "You must have cos you're still there watching this."

"No." My head finally shook as tears of horror and rage singed my eyes.

"Harley, what the fuck is going on?" Jobe hissed behind me. Rome just sat, white and silent, his acumen telling him exactly what was going on.

"Trouble is," Michael's recorded voice continued. "I know you. I taught you well, my queen." He sighed. "I think I really did love you, in my own special way. You were just a pawn in the game I had to play, princess. Your daddy, he was a mean fucker. And well, he had to pay for what he did. You were supposed to go with your family, on the same day. But don't blame me for that one. I had no control over it. And James wanted the whole family. But I thought I should have a little play with you first. Might as well have some fun, huh?" He laughed again. "But now I'm bored."

I was vibrating with rage, with fear, with undiluted vehemence and I couldn't get my brain to work.

"Get out," Rome finally spoke, his voice barely a whisper. But I heard it. I heard it as if it was as loud as a scream.

"Anyway, I digress," Michael continued. "You think I would just offer you a key tripwire? With my expertise?"

"What – the – fuck!" Jobe finally gasped in realisation as his eyes slid down to the key Rome still had pressed down hard under his finger, his knuckle white with the sheer strength he held that fucking thing down with.

Michael tutted. And then he grinned. Cruelly. Coldly. And fucking victoriously. He leaned toward the camera, his ugly fucking face growing ever nearer. "Take your pick, my Harley Queen. Trip-mine, or..." He rocked his head from side to side and clicked his tongue in rhythm, "...Time bomb?" And he winked.

His image disappeared and a photograph of my family filled his place.

With a simple timer in bold red letters.

03:00

Thirty
ROME

02:56

The silence was deafening. My mouth was so dry, my throat closing in as my heart rate escalated to accommodate the adrenaline surging through my system.

02:47

I could taste the fear pouring from Harley as she slowly stood up beside me. Her heart beat so hard I swear I could hear it within the ear-piercing wail of nothing.

02:38

"Can it...Can it be broken?" Jobe asked so quietly I wasn't sure if I'd imagined his voice.
Harley's swallow was loud. "No. It's a constant. It can't be altered, or broken down." Her tiny voice quivered and the sound of it made my heart roar in pain.

"Go," I whispered, unable to form words with the thickness of my tongue.

"No." Jobe growled. "No! We'll figure it out."

Harley was silent. She knew.

"It's unbreakable," I uttered quietly, forcing saliva into my mouth. "Go. Now."

"What about if we weigh the key down?"

"It's finger sensitive," Harley choked out, her words practically inaudible. "There isn't a way to replicate the force of a human touch. Not in three fucking minutes anyway!" She spat, her voice finally finding her.

Jobe appeared beside me, his face as pale as Harley's. "Rome." His head shook wildly, his eyes hard on mine when I pierced him with a knowing stare.

"You know what to do," I told him. "It's yours, dude. You know."

02:14

His bottom lip quivered and he grabbed at his hair, spinning and screaming into nothing. "No! Not this time!"

He moved so quickly I didn't see it coming. His finger pressed the key at exactly the same time as he pushed me out of the chair, my body skidding sideways and into the wall with the impact.

Every part of me ceased to function as horror took control.

"Get out!" Jobe screamed when the timer ticked under two minutes. "GO."

"Jobe!" I roared at him as I flew across the room.

"Get her out of here!" he snarled at me as he grounded himself over the keyboard. His eyes fixed on me, tears spilling over as he nodded to me. "It's my turn now, brother. I need to do this. You kept me safe for so many years. Now it's my turn."

Harley dropped to her knees, a desolate cry ripping from her heart and making mine shatter inside me.

"No." Every part of me bled into the room, my soul reaching out for help.

Jobe lifted his hand and cupped my face. "I love you, Rome. God, only you know how fucking much. You think I could last without you?" His head shook harder. "I would never have survived without you. You loved me so hard that I'm going with a fucking smile, brother. You loved me so hard that wherever the fuck I go, you'll be with me."

Harley crawled over to him, burying her face into the side of his neck. He turned his face and squeezed his eyes closed, inhaling her, allowing her to drug him and give him that last final high. "You take care of him," he whispered, pressing a kiss to each of her eyes.

She nodded, a choked sob torturing us all. "I love you," she breathed. "So, so much."

"I love you more, my beautiful girl." Flashing her his cheeky wink, he bit into his bottom lip. "Now get him out of here."

A cry ripped from her when she gave him one last hard kiss and then took my trembling hand.

"No," I sobbed, clinging to my brother. "I can't."

"Yes," he bit out, "Yes. You can. You love her for both of us. You laugh for both us. And you fucking live for both of us." He sucked in a breath and gritted his teeth. "Now get the fuck out of here!"

Harley tugged on my hand, her cries as loud as mine.

"GO!" Jobe screamed as the clock hit one minute. "GO!"

My feet moved as Harley pulled me across the room. My hand gripped the doorframe and I took one last look back.

00:23

Jobe smiled. And he nodded. "I'll be waiting," he mouthed. "And I'll always be with you."

I don't remember leaving the house. I don't remember the ear-splitting roar as Harley's home blew from the inside out. I don't remember the sound of my own screams.

I just remember his smile.

And I'll never forget it.

Thirty-one
HARLEY

The tiny bit of satisfaction I got as I clicked the enter key didn't last very long. My eyes lowered to it. To the key that would forever haunt me. And so I made sure to make it work for me. For Rome. For Jobe.

"Did it burrow?" Ben asked, the hope and fear in his voice making me blow out a breath.

"I think so." I watched numbers scroll, colours merge, encryptions decrypt and sizzle. Closing my eyes, I shot both Jobe and Evan a prayer. "Now I need you both," I whispered.

It had been four days. Rome was so quiet, so withdrawn. A piece of him had died, literally. He struggled to take each breath, he battled with the simplest of functions, and he watched over me every second of every day. I thought he would have shifted his grief to blame, on me. But he didn't. Although he never left my side, he made no attempt to love me. And I knew why.

"You be careful. Do not leave this fucking house," Ben growled at me as we both turned to look at Rome through the glass partition wall, perched on the sofa in his own little world.

I gave him a nod and watched him disappear through Rome's apartment door. Blowing out a nervous breath I left the office and slowly went to my man.

He didn't look at me when I came to stand in front of him, still lost to the horrors in his head.

"Is it Jobe's?"

His eyes shot up, widening and fixing on me. Shock glittered in each unique eye but then the shimmer of tears softened the pain and misery. A small smile, the first one in so long, lightened his face and he leaned forward, placing his hand over my stomach. "Yes. He was the only one who didn't use a condom."

I nodded, my mouth drying. "Why didn't you tell me?"

He shrugged, and let out a long sigh. "You were coping with the withdrawal. We weren't sure your mind could cope with it just yet."

"But…" I stutter, incoherent thought failing me. "How did you know? How did you find out?"

Sensing my worry, he slipped his hand across my stomach and grabbed my hand. "We had a doctor here. He couldn't give you medication without asking."

"If I was…pregnant?"

"Yes. He asked and, well, Jobe said he hadn't used anything. So the doctor did a blood test. Your Coco-Pops have been loaded with vitamins, and drugs, *safe drugs*, to help you and baby with the withdrawal." A mischievous twinkle in his eyes made mine water, the sight of his sheer beauty making my heart pang for another.

"Rome," I whispered.

"Carter," he corrected. "There's no more Rome and Jobe, only Carter. Two in one."

I nodded, my heart swelling at the dedication to his brother. "Carter, I'm not doing so well."

Tears dripped off my chin and landed on his face as he looked up at me. The agony on his face made me drop to my knees and bury my face into him, my arms clinging to him as if he would vanish before my eyes. "I'm not doing so good," I repeated.

"Babe," he choked out, his tears wetting my hair and bearing down on me with the weight of them. "He loved you so very much."

"I know. And he loved you more. He gave you his life, Rome...Carter. He gave you my life, and his baby's life. I need you to love us for both of you."

His cries became suffocating, his fingers digging into my flesh so hard I knew he would leave bruises. "I'm so lost, Harley," he wept. "I'm so fucking lost without him. I don't know what to do. My heart hurts, my lungs hurt, my soul is in fucking agony. I'm just so damn fucking...angry!"

I climbed onto his lap, taking his wet face in my soft hold. "I'm sorry. I'm so sorry. This all on me."

He growled, shaking his head. "Fuck. No."

He was angry. And I understood that. He was hurting more than I could help him. "Do you hate me?"

He shook his head hard, his horrified eyes finding mine. "No. Never. I'm so hateful of everything. But never you."

I slid against his crotch, trying to ease his frustration and give him any bit of pleasure and diversion I could. His cock was hard, his stare just as much so.

I ran my tongue up the side of his neck, planting tiny kisses over his skin and up to his ear. "Do you want to hate fuck me?"

He gasped, his cock hardening and pressing into my pussy. His fingers slid into my hair and he took a fistful, winding it around his knuckles and pulling my head back so he could stare into my guilty eyes. "I just want to love you," he whispered.

I scrambled with his fly, as he yanked at my jeans, tearing them down my legs just enough until I was exposed and sliding down his length. We both gasped, the pleasure driving a wedge between the hurt and pain.

Dropping his face to my chest, he clung to me as I rode him slowly and deeply, grinding my hips against his pelvis to grant him every molecule of ecstasy that I could.

"Harley," he breathed against me, using me, needing me. Loving me for both of the men I had fallen in love with.

We both fell at the same time, the need for pleasure overriding the agony and giving our souls a reprieve.

"He'll pay, I promise." And I did. I fucking swore it.

"How?" he snarled, pulling back from me. "He's been one step ahead all this time. We can't chase what we can't find, or see."

"It's okay." I took his face in my hands, my heart aching at the desolation staring back at me. "We won't need to chase him. He's coming here."

He stilled, tilting his head in confusion. "What? How?"

Running my thumb across his bottom lip, I collected his heartache and slipped it between my lips. I slid off him, pulled my jeans back up and settled on the floor in front of him. I deserved his grief and pain as much as my own. Leaning back on my heels, I stared at the floor. "A long time ago, Michael hit my equipment. Just like this time. It was different then though. He completely wiped me out, cleaned my system of everything. It was all just a game to him, and at that time he still wanted to play – with me."

Carter watched me closely, his brows pinched tight as he listened.

My mouth was so dry and I gagged subconsciously at what I had done. "Did you know my father?"

"I knew of him but not personally."

I smiled wide with the memories. "He was the best father in the world. Nothing was too much trouble for him where I was concerned. He doted on me. He was the most notorious hacker and tech guy in Britain, in fact much farther. He had men, a group that worked with him. Much like me, Evan and Ben. But much more, and a whole lot fucking wider. My dad had allies in every part of the world. He was loved, because he was the best, but not only that, he was cruel but fair, tough yet so soft with his children. And family is everything to these guys."

Carter slipped his hand in mine and squeezed tight when my past, once again, made me hurt.

"Anyway," I shook my head. "You just need to know that a lot of men owed my dad. A lot. And they're all mean fuckers. They tried to help me after my family died, but by then I had met Michael and I was too far in my own shit to allow them anything of me. To me, they were the reason my dad was dead. They should have looked out for him, protected him and my family. I was angry then, and it was all just a mess in my head."

"I get it," he said, nodding his head faintly.

"But back to Michael wiping my work." I sniffed. "Ben wrote a program afterwards. Everything on each of our systems is randomly, but frequently, uploaded to the other's personal ones, more than just the ones in my basement, as a backup. It was just to protect our work, and us."

Carter's eyes widened.

"The virus, in its procedural term, not material, was uploaded to Ben's."

Carter sat silent.

"Michael didn't bother to veil his pathway because, well, I should be dead. So Ben inverted it, and traced its channel."

"You have Michael's location?"

"No. It doesn't work like that. But it gave us an in to his kit. The doors were still open at his end. He hadn't severed the link." I was trying to be non-technical even though I suspected Carter would be able to keep up with me.

He dropped backwards, his eyes narrow but with a flare of hope, and awe. "You can hack into Michael's shit?"

I cleared my throat and shifted. "I can, and I have."

"What did you do?"

"I sent in a bot. It will work its way through and establish a connection with every single address I gave it, but it will appear as though it's come straight from Michael."

"And what is it going to do when it makes contact with each address?"

I swallowed back the nausea. "It will upload a video."

He knew. He stiffened, and blanched. "A video of what?"

I lowered my head, the heat on my face searing the air around us.

"A video of what, Harley?" His fingers curled around the tops of my arms and he yanked me up to his level. "Of what?"

"Of..." I ran my tongue around my teeth, trying in vain to lubricate them. "Of four men raping me."

My pulse was beating so hard in my ears that I nearly missed his sharp intake of breath. "You... you sent that... The horror you went through, to seek vengeance for Jobe?"

I nodded. "At this very moment, every man that was on my dad's payroll will be receiving a video of their best friend's daughter being raped and mutilated. They will also be listening to Mole explain exactly why my father was killed, and who was associated with the death of the Davids family."

His eyes grew wider and wider with every word.

"And every single associate of Michael's will right about now be accepting a delayed virus, disguised as a tasty porn film – from Michael, of course," I added with a grin. "That will clear out their bank accounts and deposit it all into one of Mr Michael McKenzie."

"So it will look like he stitched up his own friends."

I nodded slowly. "Spot on."

"So, either your father's friends will find him, or his own contacts will."

"My father's people will find him first. It'll take Michael's friends a while to figure it out, it's a delayed worm to give us time. But I don't want any backlash on my dad's friends for this."

"So you covered their backs by making Michael's upcoming murder a gift."

"Spot on," I repeated. "He knew I had the video. He knew it implicated him, and that's why he's been playing me. But he thought I wouldn't ever distribute it." I shuddered. "It's not very... complimentary." I laughed trying to hide my mortification.

"Well, yeah." Carter leaned into me, placing a soft kiss to my lips. "You should have destroyed it, Harley. I know they're your dad's friends, but fuck, to send them that, of yourself. You're hurting yourself more."

I shook my head. "They're good people, Carter. As you know, not all criminals are bad people." I shot him a cheeky wink. "For them to watch that will be like witnessing their own daughter get raped. And then the confession from Mole, and Michael's implication. They'll be out for blood."

"But you wanted to be the one," he sighed, the sadness in his eyes consuming me.

"And I will be." I grinned. "They will bring him to me as a gift."

"Shit!" Carter chuckled. "Well, fuck me. My girl is a genius."

"See," I shrugged, "There it is again! I've told you this many, many times."

"And I need to tell you time and time again how much both Jobe and I love you."

"You don't need to. I know. I'll always feel his love, in you. Because he lives on, in you." I palmed my stomach. "And in his child. *Our* child. Let him have his peace, Carter. He never found it in life. Give it to him as the last gift you can."

A single tear rolled from his eyes, and he nodded. "That I can give him."

"And, of course," I whispered. "I'll love you for the both of us. And his child will love you for who his father was, and who his daddy will be. From now, we live life for Jobe Carter. We keep breathing air for him, and we honour him in everything we do. He will never die, Rome. Because we won't let him."

Pulling me up into his lap, he hugged me close, peppering my hair with kisses from both him and his brother. I smiled. Because I was right, Jobe would never die. I felt him in the arms of Rome, I heard him in each breath that Rome exhaled. I saw him in the green and blue depths of Rome's soul.

Rome was right. Carter lived, and in him so did both Rome and Jobe.

Thirty-Two
ROME

The hitman was going to die. The anger I'd carried inside me for so many years would soon join my brother in the afterlife. Caesar044 had promised Ariel15 that we would end this. Both Jobe and I had operated as Caesar, we'd both lived as the hitman, and we'd both promised to complete the mission with the eradication of Number Four. It was the second to last promise we'd made. I would love Harley forever. I remembered back to the night Jobe died. We'd fucked Harley and she'd slipped off into the office. Jobe and I had laid on separate sofas and promised that we would love Harley forever. We made that promise as two separate men who would love one woman in entirely different, yet synchronised, ways and I would honour the pact until the day I took my last breath. But it was Carter's promise I would keep tonight. We'd also promised, before falling asleep while our girl worked her magic, that Carter would end with the death of Michael McKenzie. We would clear our accounts, shut down our operations, and disappear. And that was what I planned to do tonight, with Harley, and the baby that belonged to the three of us. Kill the cunt who had ruined our lives, and walk together into the new life that awaited us, as a pair, and not the trio we should have grown old as.

"He'll be here," I said as Harley paced in front of me. "You know he'll be here, babe."

"I know."

Still she continued to pace and I continued to watch her burn tracks in the carpet. She caressed her stomach, one hand gripping the bottom, the other caressing the top, her natural instinct to protect already soothing the tiny form inside her. I looked up at the ceiling, saying a silent prayer to my brother in the sky, that he'd get us through this with no glitches. We couldn't take anymore punishment. We were done. I'd never believed that more than when I looked at my woman—*our* woman—and noted the dark rings under her eyes, the devastation that held her features in permanent contortion, and the tension and fear of what would happen tonight that made her back bow, her legs tremble and her teeth worry her bottom lip.

"It could be days."

"It won't be days," she said, stopping to glance at me for just a minute. "He'll be here tonight."

"Will you sit down?" She shook her head. "Please. You made me promise to love you both for Jobe, which I can do without question. But, for now, the responsibility is in your hands. You can't suffer physically, because you're no longer carrying just yourself."

She stopped, her muscles going into a state of shock. When what I said sank in, she turned and faced me, smiling sadly as the tears in her eyes glimmered with sadness. They never left, the tears, but when I held her at night—when we held each other and cried over the loss of our puzzle piece—after she'd fallen asleep, I tried to kiss every one away and prayed another wouldn't follow.

"You're right." She nodded and walked towards me, tumbling into my waiting arms and curling up on my lap. "I'm sorry."

With Harley in my arms, breathing deeply, and our baby in her stomach between us, protected by the both of us, I laid us down across the sofa and stroked her hair until we both fell asleep.

Fuck. Whoever wanted into the apartment meant business. Three loud bangs on the door woke me up. Three more made me sit up and rub my eyes. The seventh, eighth and ninth bangs brought me back to life.

"Harley." I shook her gently as I stood up and jogged to the door. "Babe."

When I reached the door and turned, she was awake, standing up, and she had her game face on.

"Open the door."

I did, and no sooner had the latch loosened, the door flew open and a dude the size of the fucking doorway stormed in. Alec stood behind him and two more men flanked Alec. They were old, white-haired, rubbery and worn, but Jesus shit, the look in their eyes made my blood freeze over. I stepped back, letting them in.

"Get the merchandise," one of the guys said. The big—big*ger* one.

The second he'd spoken Harley flew into his arms and he hoisted her from the ground, burying his face in her strawberry-scented hair. A growl rumbled low in my throat but I kept it contained. Now was not the time to be possessive, or jealous of a man who exuded an uncle-like energy. Not that I would know. I no longer had a family. I stared up at the ceiling as tears blurred my vision and the sounds of Harley's sobs filled the room.

"I'm sorry," she said, finally breaking in the arms of her father's friend. "I didn't know what else to do."

"Sweetie." His voice was low and throaty, but vibrated with so much loving attention, it was impossible to ignore. This guy had been there in the beginning. "You should have come to us sooner. You know what Frank always said: Two heads are better than one, but three heads-"

"-Equal success," she finished.

Fuck. Three heads equal success. There was no longer three of us. I tried to swallow away the foreboding feeling that we were going to fail again.

"Babe?"

When I looked down from the ceiling where I'd been praying to my brother, I saw Harley staring at me. So was the big guy.

"This is my uncle, Clarke." She smiled softly. "Clarke, this is Carter. He's the love of my life and you will be nice to him."

"Carter, huh?"

I froze, conscious of every breath, every beat of my heart, every ounce of blood roaring in my veins. He knew. I knew he knew.

"Yes, sir." I nodded in respect and extended my hand to him.

"I'm sorry about your brother," he said when he took it and nodded in condolence. "Anyway..."

He clapped, making me jump, and I reached for Harley. She stepped into my arms willingly—something I didn't think I'd have ever gotten from her—and reached up to kiss my neck. My pulse spiked, the adrenaline took the invitation to join us, and when Michael was dragged in through the front door of my apartment, retribution and revenge delivered itself to us.

Thirty-Three
HARLEY

The second I saw him, I felt sick. When two of Clarke's men dragged Michael in by his elbows, I turned and threw up into one of the potted plants by the bi-fold doors. No one batted an eyelid at the woman being sick in the living room, but I felt Rome's answering wince. Like he and Jobe had been in sync, feeling everything the other one felt, Rome and I now experienced that same connection. We'd been through so much together, lost so much whilst standing side by side, that it was impossible to not know how the other one felt.

"Always were weak, Harley Queen," Michael spat, laughing at me as I righted myself. "At least you realised I'm smarter than you and called in the cavalry."

Before I could answer, Rome thrust his fist into my ex-boyfriend's face, cracking his nose. Michael's head lolled sideways, but Clarke's man held it upright.

"Why me?" I asked, taking a step towards him. "Why Jobe? Why Evan? Why any of us? You had what you wanted from me, but you still kept playing, convinced you'd win?" Another step forward. "Does it feel like you've won, Mikey? Do you see that you've made me stronger, that I'll survive and watch you die?"

"It was just too much to resist," he croaked with a smile, spitting out the blood that poured from his nose to his mouth. "You always thought you'd win. I just wanted to push until you realised you couldn't. Have you won? Really?"

"Yes, I've won. We've beat you."

"Perhaps." He grinned. Rome hit him again, splitting his lip and sending his head so far back that his neck cracked. When he'd righted himself, Michael laughed, and continued. "You don't think Jamie and I planned this?"

"What are you talking about?"

"Firstly, we gave you the ability to take two cocks at once. Your boyfriend can thank us for that." Rome growled, but he was as intrigued as I was. He was in control—for now.

"Watch your fucking mouth," Clarke said, his voice as cool as ice, calm as possible, and yet he was deadly. More dangerous than all of us.

"Secondly, Jamie and I ordered your hit, knowing Carter here would be the man to take you out."

My legs threatened to give way and I glanced at Rome. He refused to make eye contact, snarling at Michael. He took a step towards him, raising his fist to strike him again, but I grabbed his wrist. Rome might not have wanted to hear what Michael had to say, but I did.

"Oh, you didn't tell her that part?" Michael asked, antagonising Rome. "Harley, darling. Meet the man I hired to kill you. He was instructed to come to your gallery and snuff out your flame, but I knew he wouldn't do it. He's never actually taken a woman's life. Pussy." He laughed.

"You..." I choked, fighting back the tears. "You were going to kill me?"

"No." Rome shrugged, still refusing to look at me. "I wasn't going to kill you. The second you became more than a name, I ended the job and sent the money back."

"Eh, swings and roundabouts. Should I go on?" Michael asked. I nodded. "You see, we figured he'd fall for you. He isn't as strong as he makes out—Charlotte, Grant's sister, she made sure of that before he'd even become part of the plan."

I stroked my stomach, realising I was giving away too much when the nausea threatened to break me again. Saliva filled my mouth and bile burned the back of my throat. Charlotte. The woman who had broken my men, given them the final push into existing as one, had become part of Michael's game.

"What's your point?" I asked, feeling a breeze sweep over me that reminded me of Jobe.

Rome finally looked at me, and he'd felt it too. I nodded, telling him I wouldn't hold his job to kill me against him. I'd known he was dangerous when I met him, and that hadn't changed.

"My point is, he fell in love with you. You fell in love with him. I win."

"How?" I stopped Rome hitting him again. His control was wavering and I feared he'd snap before I got my answers. "How does me being happy mean you win?"

"Today, you'll move on. You'll kill me and take a victory, you'll heal and you'll live your fucking happy ever after. But he'll die. He has made so many enemies, stolen from so many men, and scorned many women and children. One day, he'll be taken from you and all of my hard work will be revealed. Old wounds will be torn open. The festering hole I've left in your soul will eat you alive…and you'll be done. And by that point, you'll have no Carter to keep you safe from yourself."

"You're lying," I said, clenching my fists to keep the feeling in my fingers.

Then I stepped away from him. Clarke looked on, wondering if I was crazy—if I was going to break. The two men holding Michael on his knees looked at me. The two men guarding Alec at the door looked at me.

Rome looked at me.

Only the look in his dazzling eyes told me he believed Michael. I wouldn't allow Rome to be taken from me. From us. I would spend the rest of my life readying to lay my existence down to save him and our baby.

"So you see, I win because I gave you love. And love is the only weapon that can truly ruin us." He took a deep breath and mimicked the sound of an explosion, making me double over and cry in realisation when the grief I felt at Jobe's loss stabbed through me. Michael was right.

"No."

I looked up at Rome and saw him standing in front of Michael, his stance dominating and confident. He had become Carter, channelling a little bit of Jobe's crazy in order to hurt Michael.

"See, you're wrong. Am I going to spout you with romantic bullshit and grant you more breaths while you listen to exactly why you're wrong? No." He cleared his throat. I watched on with a racing heart. "But I'll tell you this...you underestimated me. I've made all the preparations to keep Harley, and our baby, safe. All you've really done is give two people the happiness they deserve. And while one of us will die first, it's true, we've got plenty of years and heads of grey hair ahead of us. And we'll grow that hair, we'll fuck every night, we'll laugh, we'll cry and we'll find the happiness you don't deserve, all while you rot in the ground and keep the circle of life going. You lose, mate. You lost the minute you let Harley go."

God, I loved him. I loved him so fucking much. Sure, we didn't have forever. We knew that...but we had now, and we had tomorrow and the next day, and as many days as we were granted while Rome and Jobe's precautions kept us safe.

"Babe," Rome called, nodding for me to join him. When I stopped next to him, he reached into his pocket and handed me a small knife. "Cut your name in his skin."

"W-what?"

"Brand him. Make sure the fucking underworld knows his death belongs to you."

My breath became sharp and short, the lack of oxygen making my head fuzz and my vision blur. But I took the knife. I took it, remembering seeing it in Rome's kitchen, and glanced down at it in my palm. Closing my fist around the handle, I looked at Rome.

"Clarke, would you please ask your man to hand me his gun?" I gasped. This was really happening. "I'm also going to need my laptop."

Silence greeted him, including from me. I just stared between the knife and the love of my life, wondering if I could do this. I had promised my dead family revenge. I had promised to avenge Evan's death, and I had a duty to punish the man who had stolen my baby's biological father from me. I could do this. I would do this. As soon as Rome had what he'd asked for.

"Don't just stand there," Clarke said, clapping his hands and licking his lips in excitement. He turned to Rome. "Can we trust your doorman?" Rome nodded without hesitation. Clarke gestured to the men either side of Alec and they stepped away. "Get Carter what he asked for!"

They scurried off, looking at me for direction when it came to the laptop and I directed them to his office. When they returned, Rome set up, opening up his laptop on the counter, pointing to a spot on the floor and instructing Clarke's men where to place Michael. They dragged him, kicking, screaming and bleeding, to the rug in the middle of the room. I stopped at the edge, remembering when I'd scrunched my toes on it not so long ago, when Jobe took me to the apartment and asked me to beg.

"Ready, babe?" Rome asked.

I nodded. I had no idea what he was going to do, but I knew what he expected me to do and I trusted him.

Thirty-Four
ROME

The first of Michael's screams echoed around the apartment and pierced my ears as I knelt on the ground at the coffee table and opened my laptop. I smiled, glancing over my shoulder at Harley as she crouched in front of Michael and, after seeking affirmation from her uncle, cut the first line of the H into his chest. He shook, blood oozing out of the cut and dripping to the waistband of his jeans. He kicked his legs out, trying to swipe at her, but Clarke's men did their job and jumped in to hold him down. She would do this. She would hesitate and that would only hurt Michael more, but she'd sworn to do it, and I refused to take over and let her suffer the regret when we couldn't undo the damage and try again.

Instead I logged in and did my thing to the soundtrack of Michael McKenzie's agony. I smiled when I hit the jackpot, hacking into Charlotte's webcam as she stepped into her bedroom and tossed her handbag onto the bed. When I whistled, she jumped and stared at the screen. Her eyes connected with the camera and I smiled, waving at her as another wail pierced the air.

"Hey…" she said, taking a step closer and narrowing her eyes on me. "Jobe?"

I growled when I heard her say his name. Stupid bitch. She'd never been able to tell the difference, relying on us to hint at which twin she was fucking when she'd been playing us.

"No."

"God, I'm sorry, Rome. How did you-"

"I'll give you the money you need," I said cutting her off.

Michael screamed again, his voice breaking as the decibels of his cry threatened to smash the glass. Charlotte craned her neck to see what was going on, like watching from a different angle would give her a view of the room.

"What's going on?"

"Do you want to get high?"

"What are you talking about?"

It all made sense. Charlotte had dabbled in cocaine when we were together and I'd been able to brush it off as the recreational drug everyone was doing. Her being hooked on it went a long way to explaining why she was still as crazy as they came and in such huge debt. She and Gareth had always done it together and the debt was more than his. She didn't want to have to pay it off, so she'd landed on my doorstep in the hopes I'd pay her dealers off and fund her fucking habit. No such luck.

That, and we couldn't afford to leave loose ends. Charlotte was not only a liability, but she was also part to blame for Jobe's death, because once upon a time she had undone all my hard work. He'd loved her more than I did. It all went back to drugs.

"Don't bullshit me, babe," I said, licking my lips like she'd always liked. "Come on, get high with me."

"So you want us to do some coke together and then you'll settle my debt? Just like that?"

I shrugged. She wouldn't resist. "Just like that."

She did think about it, buying me enough time to look over my shoulder and watch Harley. She was covered in blood, seeping from each of the three letters of her name branded into Michael's flesh, but finally she was confident. She finally understood why she needed to see her name marked on him before we killed him. I was proud of my girl. My crazy little killer. I was proud of everything she'd become when it would have been much easier to become Charlotte.

"I paid you a little visit earlier," I said when she said nothing in response to my challenge. "Check in your top drawer. The one where you keep your dildo."

She blushed and looked around the room, her gaze falling on the drawer Jace had planted my gift in earlier.

"You've been here?"

"I've been there. Guess I can't resist you. Come on, babe, I've got customers waiting."

"Forty thousand?" she asked, standing from the chair and crossing the room.

Michael had stopped screaming now. His body had gone into shock and his mind had shut down to block the pain out.

"Keep going, babe," I said to Harley, before turning to Clarke. "I'm going to need some ice water."

"You got it. You sure this is going to work?"

Clarke knew what I was doing. He was, after all, the best, and I figured it extended further than hacking email accounts.

"Cocaine and money, baby?" Charlotte caught my attention and I turned to see her at her desk, flapping a wad of cash in one hand and a little bag of cocaine in the other.

"It's good stuff." I began lining up my imaginary cocaine, rolling up a twenty where she could see it, and ducking lower. "Ready?"

"Ready."

She frowned when she looked past me, paling when she saw the organised chaos happening on the rug in my living room.

I snorted my imaginary line. Charlotte followed.

I snorted my second imaginary line. Charlotte dipped below the webcam and the sound of her sniffing filtered through the speakers.

I snorted my third imaginary line. Charlotte groaned and followed suit.

"Had enough?" I asked, pausing above imaginary line number five.

"Have you?"

"I could do this in my sleep, babe. I just want to make sure you can keep up. I want you high as a fucking kite and then I want you to get in a taxi, naked, and make your way here so I can fuck you 'til you pass out."

"Oh, I can do that," she said, snorting line number five.

"Rome..."

Harley was behind me, and placed a bloody hand on my shoulder, the knife dangling over my chest.

"Done?"

"It's done. He's not dead, though."

"Superficial cuts. They won't kill him." I kissed her hand and flicked the knife out of her grasp, onto the rug. "Give me two minutes." I turned back to Charlotte. "You've got enough for two more lines there. Finish them off and get your tight little ass here so I can fuck it into next week. You've got half hour, babe, or the deal is off."

I snapped the laptop shut and turned to Harley, inspecting her carefully and holding her at arm's length. Clarke watched over us, something in the way he stared at me telling me he didn't completely trust me, but he had asked his men to follow my commands. Buckets of iced water sat lined up on the kitchen counter.

"Are you okay?" I asked, cupping her face and cleaning her cheek from a smudge of blood.

"Yes. That was..."

"Just like riding a high."

"Yes."

"I knew you'd like it. You can't become addicted to killing people, I'm kinda tired of running, but you can remember this high forever. You'll never crave cocaine again after that."

"Clever move," Clarke said, slapping his hand on my shoulder. "Harley, we've got somewhere we need to be. Carter, do you have a cleaner?"

"I have a cleaner. We're good."

"Clarke-" Harley moved to embrace her uncle, but he shook his head and halted her. "Evidence. Sorry."

"We'll make sure all tracks are covered. Carter, keep her safe, keep in touch with me, and for the love of God, don't screw up the cover-up."

"I've got this."

Of course I did. I would not let one single thing happen to my girl. I wouldn't let Michael come back to haunt us. But he wasn't dead…yet.

Clarke and his men left, as did Alec, who had seen shit much worse than a little live-carving, until it was just Harley, Michael and me in the apartment. Michael had passed out. The wheezy breaths as blood dripped from his face to his chest to mix with those wounds and flow over to his waist were the only sign that he was alive.

"Come with me," I said, taking Harley's hand and leading her out onto the balcony.

Thirty-Five
HARLEY

It was cold outside, the chilly breeze swirling around us in-time with the bass from the club below us. Rome led me to the railing and stood behind me with his chin on my shoulder.

"My mother died eventually," he said. "I guess she couldn't take the high anymore and when her veins were shot to shit, her mind nothing but weeds that had probably once bloomed in something, she killed herself. She'd been chasing the high forever and in the end, no amount of drugs was enough to bring euphoria. So she ended it."

"Rome."

"Jobe and I already existed as Carter by that point. She hadn't noticed that she had just the one kid, while the other one hid away to let the other one live. But she wasn't the final nail in the coffin. The abuse ended when she died and we went back to being Rome and Jobe. Until-"

"Charlotte."

I hated that she'd broken them before I could love them. I hated that she was some messed up part of this, and Jobe's 'one', although he would never live to learn he deserved so much better than her. She was Gareth's brother, who was Michael's friend, who was partners with the man who had ordered the murder on my family. And she was the only person left who had sat on the game-board and had a hand in the fate we'd been handed.

"Yes, Charlotte," Rome said, as if the mere mention of her name reminded him of the heartbreak he'd suffered. "She embarrassed us. We were mortified and, for the only time in our life, we fought. Jobe wanted her, but I wanted her. Jobe loved her, but I loved her."

"But you didn't."

"No, we didn't."

"So...?"

Rome extended his arm over the balcony and pointed at the city below. A woman climbed out of a taxi and looked up at us, waving when she saw Rome.

"Turns out, she's our mother all over again. She takes anything going because she can't bear to be alone. Nor can she bear to be...less of a cunt."

"What did you do?"

He shrugged. "You reminded me that deals are arranged online. So I hacked her computer, found the abusive messages from her dealer, and then contacted him and told him the deal...that she'll never be able to pay, and that her brother, the man on Mole's payroll, was dead. His money wasn't coming in."

"So-"

A flash lit up the street before the sound of a gunshot filled the space, and the woman Rome had pointed out as Charlotte fell to the ground. Cars screeched to a halt, women screamed. A woman had been killed, shot at point blank range, on the streets of London.

"Is she..."

"Dead? Yes. Consider my demons exorcised. Now." He took hold of my shoulders and turned me to face the living room. "It's time to get rid of yours."

With a gentle nudge, he pushed me back into the room. I stood in front of Michael as Rome lifted bucket after bucket of water and poured them on the man passed out on the carpet. He coughed and spluttered, shaking his head and wincing when he woke up and remembered the pain.

"Are you done?" he groaned. "You're going to kill me anyway."

"I am," I said, falling to my knees and rolling him onto his back. "I'm going to kill you for my mother, my father and my brother. I'm going to kill you for Evan. I'm going to kill you for the Carter twin you stole from me. I'm going to kill you for the Carter brother you left alive. I'm going to kill you for me. And I'm going to kill you for my baby."

I straddled him, keeping my knees tight to his waist as I wrapped both hands around his neck. I wouldn't kill him with a gun; I wouldn't let him get out that easily. I wanted to feel the life drain from him. I wanted to feel the pain become him. I wanted to feel him give up, like he'd made me do. I wanted to feel everything.

A warm body slotted behind mine and two arms covered mine. Rome covered my hands with his and applied pressure, using his weight and physical strength to aid me in the murder. Michael tried to fight, but he was weak. His blood spread as his heart fought to keep beating, and it soaked into my clothes. It coated me in red, filled my nostrils with copper and made my heart swell with pride. Michael had stolen so much from both of us and, like Jobe and Rome shared their love for me, Rome and I shared the knowledge that we'd ended the man who ruined it all.

Rome held me for every second of a strangling that felt impossible. It felt like the minutes turned into hours, until blood vessels in Michael's eyes popped, his lips swelled, his skin turned blue, and with a final gasp, he died.

And it was over.

Epilogue
ROME

I held her hand through every second. I'd driven us to the clinic while her hand held onto my thigh. The second we'd jumped out of the car, she slipped her hand in mine and locked our fingers together. When we sat in the waiting room, I slipped my arm around her and read a baby magazine—a fucking baby magazine—with her. She chose pushchairs and highchairs and bottles with built-in bibs. She picked out cute dummies, noticed deals on nappies and baby wipes, and asked me if I would take her shopping at the weekend. Of course I fucking would.

You see, Jobe and I had even shared a family. Sure, he had conceived the child, but I would raise it. He would be the dad the child only ever heard stories about, and I would be the daddy the child would make new memories with. And through it all Harley was the constant. She was the only person who had accepted us for everything we'd done, and everything we were, and she loved us in spite of it. No. She loved us *because* of it.

"Ms Davids?" the midwife called, smiling at us as we stood. I made a mental note to change her last name to my own very, very fucking soon.

Harley deposited the magazine and we followed the nurse through the corridor.

She let us into a room and we took our seats. While hiding the pregnancy from Harley, she hadn't been for official check-ups and scans. Jobe and I had fed her folic acid, slipped vitamins into her milk, and prayed the effects of cocaine withdrawal wouldn't take them both from us. So now it was over, now we could plan for a child with no risk of being blown up; now we could move on, and that began with an appointment with the midwife.

"If you want to just jump on the bed, I'll be back in a minute," the midwife said, after taking Harley's blood pressure and pricking her finger and checking her blood sugar levels. I watched as Harley stripped, hating that even here, I wanted to take her.

"Stop it," she chastised, smiling over at me as she thrust her hands behind her head.

The midwife returned with a machine and bottle of gel. My heart clenched, knowing our baby was in there. A real baby, Jobe's baby, my baby. How fucking messed up but perfect had it turned out?

When the midwife had squirted gel onto the wand, she pressed it to Harley's stomach and turned the machine on.

"Oh my," she breathed, as the sound of a heartbeat filled the room, and tears filled Harley's eyes.

Ba-dum.
Ba-dum.
Ba-dum.
Ba-dum. Ba-dum.

Ba-dum. Ba-dum.
Ba-dum. Ba-dum.

"Well," the midwife said after 'hmm'ing for what felt like forever, while she squished Harley's stomach, restricting my baby's living space. "Congratulations." She placed the wand back and handed Harley a wad of tissue to clean the gel off her stomach.

When she turned the screen to face us, Harley gripped my hand and choked on a sob. I gasped and felt my eyes well when we glanced at the grainy image. The midwife beamed, pointing her index finger to first one spot on the screen, and then a second.

"You're having twins."

The End

86400
Seconds

**An Intense Dark Thriller
By Rebecca Sherwin
&
D H Sidebottom**

The day I died began with a sharp rush of breath and a fierce thud of my heart against my ribcage. A heavy sheen of sweat that clung to every millimetre of my icy skin, and the scent of decay in my nostrils so raw that I knew I'd never smell purity again.

The last twenty-four hours were a blur, a void in my memories. Where there should have been joyful memories of my twenty fifth birthday, a gaping hole of nothing now prevailed. Like an eraser had moved across my mind and scrubbed away yesterday as though it had never come and gone.

But I'd never forget the next twenty-four hours. The terrifying rush of the next one thousand, four hundred and forty minutes. The swiftly fading eighty-six thousand, four hundred seconds filled with the remaining twenty-eight thousand breaths of my life.

Because that's all he gave me.

Eighty-six thousand and four hundred seconds to play his game.

Eighty-six thousand and four hundred seconds to complete his five tasks before it would all blissfully end.

Each one took a piece of me until by the conclusion of his cruel self-made amusement only the slow, reluctant beat of my heart remained. Nothing else of me was left.

And then, finally, my finishing task.
Embrace death.
And embrace I did. Willingly.

Coming late autumn 2016

Caged
Erotic Thriller
By D H Sidebottom

Judd Asher was taken from his front garden when he was just four years old. After an extensive search he was never found.

Twenty-one years after a random call out, Judd is found chained and beaten in the basement of an old rundown farmhouse where he has lived the life of an animal for the last twenty-one years.

Kloe Grant is assigned as Judd's personal therapist. It's her job to rehabilitate him, to guide him back to normal life. But as Judd's only emotion is rage, Kloe finds it both heart-breaking and challenging mending a soul that's not only broken but caged inside him by the demons of his past.

However, when Kloe's relationship with her patient raises some eyebrows, Kloe can't fight against the powers that want to see her fail, and with an arm behind her back, she walks away, leaving behind a man who has come to live life again for her.

Four years later Judd, now known as Anderson Cain, the darkest and most formidable cage fighter in a world where violence and crime are the only way to keep breathing, Judd finds there's not a lot in life that can abate the rage that still twists and prowls beneath his skin.

Not until a chance encounter brings him to ***her*** door. To the woman with the bluest eyes and the most stunning smile, the woman who took his hand in the darkness and led him through the door into the sun.

But Kloe Grant left him when he needed her the most. She took the only shred of hope and trust he had left and annihilated it. She starved his belief, and she fed his fury.

She owes him. And he's going to make sure that this time, she pays. In blood. In lust. In pain. And with her soul.

Buy Now

US: http://amzn.to/1RvhHDp

UK: http://amzn.to/1RSNhgq

CA: http://amzn.to/1X5ABRz

AUS: http://bit.ly/1X5AFAA

SPOTIFY PLAYLIST: http://spoti.fi/1SHMlYZ

GRIT Sector 1: Elias
By
Rebecca Sherwin

I thought I was safe.
I FOUGHT TO KEEP THEM ALIVE.
I thought I was good.
THERE WAS NO GOOD LEFT HERE.
I thought I was just a girl.
I WAS MORE THAN JUST A MAN.
I didn't see it coming.
I SHOULD HAVE SEEN IT COMING.
Destiny had brought us together.
HISTORY WOULD TEAR US APART.

Twenty-first century London - daytime
Freedom is non-existent.
Self-expression is confined to sunlight hours.
Happiness is on a schedule.
Safety is a temporary fixture.

Twenty-first century London - nighttime.
Blood cascades over cobbled stones.
Criminals emerge from the shadows.
The depraved, the deviant, the morally corrupt, own the streets.
Happiness comes in the form of final breaths.
Safety is found in the shrills of death.

A love story emerges inside the barricades.
A story played out many times before...
But not like this.
It's evolution of tradition.
It's insanity fighting to break the cycle.
It's history's repetition with hope for a better outcome.

Can love survive in a drowning capital?
What if the good guys aren't the good guys?
What if the heroes have become the villains?

Trixie Ashford has been living a lie.
Elias Blackwood has been creating it.

It is their destiny to meet.
It will be their downfall to fall in love...

Amazon US:
https://amzn.com/B01FPTHULW
Amazon UK:
https://www.amazon.co.uk/dp/B01FPTHULW

Printed in Great Britain
by Amazon